LEILANI'S HERO

BROTHERHOOD PROTECTORS HAWAII
BOOK TWO

ELLE JAMES

TWISTED PAGE INC

LEILANI'S HERO

BROTHERHOOD PROTECTORS HAWAII
BOOK #2

New York Times & USA Today
Bestselling Author

ELLE JAMES

Dedicated to my sister because I love her.
Elle James

AUTHOR'S NOTE

Enjoy other military books by Elle James

Brotherhood Protectors Hawaii
Kalea's Hero (#1)
Leilani's Hero (#2)
Kiana's Hero (#3)
Maliea's Hero (#4)
Emi's Hero (#5)
Sachie's Hero (#6)
Kimo's Hero (#7)
Alana's Hero (#8)
Nala's Hero (#9)
Mika's Hero (#10)

Visit ellejames.com for more titles and release dates
Join her newsletter at
https://ellejames.com/contact/

CHAPTER 1

AUGUST 2023

LEILANI KEALOHA LAID down her paintbrush and stretched. She'd been working on this particular painting since early that morning and was close to finishing it, but she hadn't stopped for lunch. For the past hour, the increasing scent of smoke had her concerned. She'd checked the latest report on wildfires burning east of Lahaina. At one point, the firefighters had reported the fires had been contained. By the smell, Leilani wasn't so sure.

As she left her upstairs studio and descended the stairs from her apartment to the gallery below, the muffled, mechanical sound of a voice over a megaphone barely penetrated the walls and the large glass windows on the front of the gallery.

"Olina? Did you hear that?" she called out as she reached the bottom of the stairs and entered the back of the gallery. "What are they saying?"

Her friend, Olina, was a thirty-one-year-old single mother of three. She was the one person Leilani trusted to run the gallery while Leilani worked, creating beautiful paintings of the land and people she loved in Hawaii.

Olina wasn't in the back of the shop, nor was she behind her desk in the middle of the gallery.

Leilani glanced out the front store windows. Her friend stood on the sidewalk in front of the gallery, her hand pressed to her cheek as a city police vehicle passed slowly, the officer making an announcement over his loudspeaker.

Leilani's heart beat faster as she made out the word *evacuate*. She hurried toward the front of the gallery, arriving at the door as Olina dove through it.

"I have to go," she said in a rush.

"What's going on?" Leilani asked. "I thought they had the fires contained."

"Apparently not." Olina shook her head and ran for her desk, where she grabbed her purse and fished out her car key. "The fire has almost reached the edge of town. It sounds bad. The police are announcing that everyone in Lahaina needs to evacuate immediately." Her forehead creased in a worried frown. "I have to get to my kids. They're home alone. They won't know what to do, where to go..."

Leilani twisted the lock on the front door. "I'm going with you." She ran to catch up with Olina, who had already exited the back of the building and was climbing into the older model Mazda sedan that always seemed to be held together by sheer will and bubble gum.

Leilani paid Olina more than she could really afford, but it wasn't enough on an island with a high cost of living. Tourism had driven up the costs of housing, food and fuel to the point the locals could barely afford to live on the island their ancestors had inhabited for centuries.

Leilani had the advantage of inheriting a short row of buildings along Front Street from her grandfather. One of the buildings housed her gallery and apartment. Beside the gallery was their tour office, selling guided hiking tours and boat excursions to favorite snorkeling spots or sunset sailing trips on the catamaran.

Meanwhile, other locals like Olina and her children lived in government apartments not far from the gallery, eking out a living in the service industry catering to tourists.

Whether it was climate change or just a run of bad luck, Maui had experienced extremely dry weather, turning the vegetation into tinder, ripe for the potential of fire.

When Hurricane Dora had passed close to the chain of islands, it had stirred up such strong winds that local schools had closed. The children had been told to stay home. Many, like Olina's three kids, were alone, their parents having to go to work. Olina's oldest daughter, Mamo, was capable of watching out for her younger siblings, but she might not be aware of the encroaching danger of fire bearing down on their community.

Leilani jumped into the passenger seat and buckled her seatbelt.

Olina turned the key in the ignition and pumped the accelerator with her foot. The engine turned over once but didn't start.

After Olina's third attempt to start the engine, Leilani reached for her seatbelt buckle.

Olina tried once more. This time, the engine turned over, engaged and roared to life. The mother of three whipped the gear shift into reverse, backed out of the parking space, drove around the side of the building and met a wall of cars on Front Street, inching along, bumper to bumper. Smoke billowed over the tops of roofs, rising high into the air. When the line of cars stopped, people got out of their vehicles and stood looking to the east, shaking their heads.

"I'll go ask them what's going on," Leilani said.

Olina shook her head. "This can't be happening."

Leilani hopped out of Olina's car and ran up to the first man she came to, standing beside his vehicle. "Why is everyone stopped?"

The man turned with his cell phone to his ear. "The wind knocked power lines over onto the highway. The police blocked the road to keep people from running over live lines."

Leilani's gaze followed the dark cloud of smoke hovering ominously over the rooftops. "How are we supposed to evacuate the town if the road is blocked?"

"Good question." He looked behind him to where other vehicles blocked any chance of him turning around and heading in the opposite direction.

Leilani hurried back to Olina, who was getting out of her car.

"I can't wait for them to move," Olina said. "I see flames, and they're getting closer." She took off, running toward the apartment complex several blocks from the gallery, heading toward the smoke and flames.

Leilani kept pace with the other woman. By the time they reached the apartment, people were pouring out of the building into the street. Women carried small children. Older kids carried younger siblings. Old people moved as quickly as their frail bodies could manage.

Just as they reached the structure, Olina's three children emerged, herded out by a police officer.

"Oh, thank God." Olina ran for and engulfed her kids in a tight group hug.

The youngest child, Noa, coughed, tears slipping

down his cheeks. "The policeman said we had to get out of our house."

"Where do we go?" Eight-year-old Palili looked up at her mother, her big brown eyes rounded and worried.

"Mom, we have to get out of here." Mamo, the oldest daughter, looked around Olina. "Where's the car?"

Olina scooped Noa up into her arms. "The roads are blocked. We had to get out of here on foot."

Leilani took Palili's hand. "Come on, we have to move fast. The fire is getting closer. I don't think we can get out of town fast enough. But, if we hurry, we can make it to the water."

Already, Leilani could feel the heat as the fire bore down on Lahaina. She prayed they had enough time to get the children to the ocean. "Run!" she yelled and took off, running as fast as Palili's little legs could go.

With heat searing her back, Leilani finally grabbed Palili and swung her up into her arms. The little girl wrapped her arms and legs around Leilani and held on tight as they ran with others toward Lahaina Harbor.

After her first terrifying glance back at the flames leaping high into the sky from the roofs of homes and businesses, Leilani focused on the path ahead. Looking back would only slow them down. They had to make it to the water before the fire caught up to them.

As she passed others, looking lost and indecisive, Leilani yelled, "Head for the water!"

The heat intensified to the point Leilani felt as if she were being baked in an oven. Drenched in sweat, she blinked to keep the salty moisture from burning her eyes. Passing between buildings, she could barely see through the haze darkening the sky. Her lungs burned from breathing hard, every breath filling them with the thick, smoky air. Burning embers fell from the sky, carried from the fire through the air by hefty gusts of wind.

"Have to make it to the water," she murmured, unsure of her direction as she fought for each step.

"There!" Olina cried.

Through the billowing smoke, Leilani glimpsed the harbor ahead.

As she neared the water, the embers landed on her, burning her skin. She didn't hesitate, running into the cool Pacific Ocean and wading in all the way up to her waist before easing the weight of the child in her arms.

"Stay close together," Olina called out.

Leilani moved closer to Olina, Mamo and Noa, the waves and current threatening to carry her further out.

She stared toward the boat slips, wondering if they could make it to one of her boats. Even if they did, she didn't have keys to start an engine.

Finally, she turned to look at the shore, her heart

sinking low in her belly. The town that had been home her entire life was a raging inferno. Flames licked the dark clouds, flinging fiery embers into the air, igniting a car, cooking through the paint, melting the tires and...

Boom!

The gas tank exploded, sending shrapnel and flaming fuel through the air.

Leilani ducked lower in the water to avoid the burning embers. "Hold on, Palili. I won't let go of you."

"I'm scared," she said, her arms wrapping tightly around Leilani's neck.

Mamo and Olina, holding Noa, edged closer.

"I'm right here," Olina said. "We're safe out here. They'll send people out to help us."

"When, mommy?" Noa asked, his teeth chattering, his little body shivering in the cool water.

"We have to be patient," Olina said. "It might take a while, but they'll come."

The heated air did nothing to warm their bodies below the surface. The chill soon spread through Leilani. She moved around to keep blood circulating and hugged Palili's body close to share what little body warmth each could generate.

"I'm cold," Noa said.

"I know, baby," Olina said. "We all are." She moved closer to Leilani and Palili. Mamo did as well until they pressed against each other.

Other people floated in the water nearby. A couple of teen boys rubbed their mother's arms to keep her warm.

Leilani tried to think of anything else but how cold she was and how long she'd been in the water. She looked toward the shore, tears filling her eyes. The buildings that had been in her family for decades were quickly disappearing into a molten glob of fire.

"Your work," Olina exclaimed.

"Not important," Leilani assured her. She smiled into Palili's face. "Family is what matters. I'm glad we were able to get to your babies before..."

Olina nodded, tears slipping from her eyes, leaving tracks through the sooty dust coating her cheeks. "We were lucky," she said softly, her gaze meeting Leilani's. "So many kids were home alone."

Leilani chest ached. They'd barely had time to get to Olina's kids and rush them into the water. What about the others?

She wanted to go back and look for more members of her community, but she couldn't leave the ones with her. The current could easily sweep Palili's light body away.

Flying embers landed on some of the boats moored at the jetty, setting them on fire.

Leilani couldn't think about the loss of her businesses, her paintings, the art studio she'd loved equipping with empty canvasses, brushes, an easel and all the shades of oil paint and watercolor palettes. She'd been working on a commissioned painting for Washington Place, the governor's mansion located in downtown Honolulu. She'd been so close to finishing. Now...gone.

As the fire consumed Leilani's studio and gallery, she sighed. Better to have lost the painting than the lives of her friend Olina and her precious children.

For what seemed like forever, they stood in the cool water, buffeted by wind and waves, holding onto the hope that someone would come to their rescue.

Cold and exhausted, Leilani focused on holding herself together. She couldn't let Palili know how hopeless she felt at that moment. When would help come?

Leilani fought to stay awake when all she wanted was to slip beneath the surface and sleep.

Drowning wasn't an option—a possibility, maybe, but not a choice. Palili needed Leilani to focus on survival. Things could be replaced. People could not.

The fire burned through the night, warming the air coming from that direction. The slight lightening of the sky heralded morning.

Leilani blinked several times and tossed her hair. A horn sounded. Through the smoke, she caught glimpses of a Coast Guard cutter moving slowly, the crew plucking survivors from the water.

Leilani's pointed. "They're here."

Olina hugged Noa so tightly he squirmed. When she raised her head, tears streamed down her cheeks.

Noa planted his hands on each side of her face and stared into her eyes. "Mommy, why are you crying?"

Olina laughed. "These are happy tears. I'm happy I have all of you with me."

As the cutter moved closer, Leilani's eyes welled, the tears spilling over and running down her face.

"Ms. Lani." Palili stared into her face. "It's going to be all right. They're coming to save us."

"Like your mama said, these are happy tears." Leilani hugged Palili close, knowing how close they'd been to death.

One by one, they were lifted into the cutter, wrapped in blankets and handed warm cocoa poured from a thermos.

Leilani had never tasted anything so good, letting the chocolate-flavored liquid warm her insides. When she asked to borrow a cell phone, one of the rescue workers shook his head. "Cell phone towers are out. No service. We're transmitting data via radio to our operations center."

They gave their names to be relayed to whoever was collecting information about survivors.

As the sun rose over Maui, the smoke lifted enough to reveal the smoldering remains of what had once been a thriving community.

Leilani settled Palili, Olina, Noa and Mamo inside the cutter and headed back out onto the deck to help other survivors as they were brought aboard the cutter. Between rescues, she stared broken-heartedly at what looked like the aftermath of a bombed-out warzone, not the beautiful town she remembered.

In the place of the lush green trees stood blackened sticks. Where buildings once stood were beds of ashes and the outlines of what had been foundations. The boats that hadn't made it out of the harbor were burned and sunk, only a handful surviving intact.

As she helped people who'd been fished out of the water, she recognized some as employees, family and friends.

Had Richard Ako, one of the boat captains, tried to get to the boats before the fires had reached the harbor? If so, had he gotten his wife and children out safely first? What about Josh Wright, her favorite deckhand or Makai Kealoha, her cousin and his fiancée? She searched soot-covered faces and prayed for the ones she didn't see.

For hours, private boat owners assisted the Coast Guard in retrieving people from the water or near the shore. Survivors were transported to evacuation shelters where they had access to food, medical care, showers, cots to sleep on and donated clothing.

Leilani moved in a daze, helping where she could and taking care of her own personal needs. Through it all, the haunted faces of locals and visitors were seared into her memory. Some cried, others sat in stunned silence. People had lost loved ones, family pets, everything they owned.

Exhausted from staying awake all night in the cold water, Leilani pulled a cot close to Olina's family and laid down for the first time in over forty-eight hours,

She wanted to go home, crawl into her own bed and sleep through this nightmare.

In that moment, the realization truly sank in. She didn't have a home to go to. She'd lost everything, like so many others. The life she'd known, the buildings that had been her family's for as long as she could remember, were gone. Her paintings, family photos...gone.

Tears leaked from the corners of her eyes as she lay on her cot. She'd been a planner, someone who'd had control of her life and a clear path to her future.

The fire had ripped all that stability, years of building her business as an artist, carrying on the family tourist business out from under her.

She lay for a long time, staring up at the high gymnasium ceiling, wondering where to start, how to rediscover who Leilani Kealoha was without the comfort of her past, her heritage or her life in Lahaina.

The sheer magnitude of change threatened to overwhelm her. For several minutes, her heart raced, and her breathing grew labored as a panic attack swept over her. Taking over a thriving family business and building it even bigger was nothing compared to starting from scratch. She'd never done that and wasn't sure she could.

Soft whimpers and sobs from others in the vast gym reminded her she wasn't the only one faced with starting over.

No matter how devastating her losses, she had survived. Her responsibility was to build back so much of what she'd lost. The people who worked for her depended on the businesses to support their families.

Rising from the ashes wasn't just about her losses but helping her people get back on their feet.

Not only did Olina depend on her, but Noa, Palili and Mamo depended on her, as well as other employees and their families.

But right that moment, she couldn't think past how tired she was. She'd sleep. When she woke, she'd get on with the task of rebuilding her businesses and helping her community through this tragedy.

Leilani would do this.

She had no other choice.

CHAPTER 2

Four months later

"WHAT WAS wrong with staying at the resort and enjoying the pool and drinks?" Devlin asked.

Angelo Cortez, aka Angel, frowned. "You don't learn much about Maui by staying on a resort. Though Hawk told us to enjoy a little R&R before we report to the Big Island, it behooves us to do a little exploring on the other islands, including the one we're on."

"Especially if our work involves security or protection of people on the other islands," Teller agreed. "We need to understand the lay of the land, hiding places, ingress and egress points. We may need to access one or all of them at some time during our assignments."

"Speaking of assignments, have any of you heard anything?" Reid leaned against the side of the building, dressed in khaki slacks and a white polo shirt, his only fashion digression the sturdy hiking boots.

Angel guessed the man had a Speedo bathing suit under the pants. The former Navy SEAL rarely missed an opportunity to get in the water, even if it was standing in the rain.

Having grown up on South Padre Island, Texas, Angel felt the same. He had joined the Navy with every intention of becoming a Navy SEAL to be in the water more than on a ship. He'd worked hard to attain that elite status. Ironically, he'd spent most of his Navy SEAL career performing missions in the deserts of the Middle East or in land-locked countries of Africa.

Angel, Reid Bennet, Devlin Mulhaney and Teller Osgood stood outside the Swaying Palm Resort on Maui, waiting for the tour bus that would take them to three of Maui's most famous waterfalls. Yes, they could have taken the rental car and gone on their own, but having a local tour guide ensured they'd get a little more history and cultural background.

A group of senior citizens gathered near the shuttle bus Angel assumed would take them to the trailheads. Most sported gray hair, wide-brimmed hats and long-sleeved shirts to cover thinning skin. They laughed and joked among themselves, making

Angel smile. He planned to be as active at their age, still traveling and exploring the world.

A young, dark-haired woman wearing a sky-blue polo shirt with the Windsong Tours logo embroidered on the left breast emerged from the resort front entrance, carrying a clipboard.

She couldn't be more than five feet tall and probably didn't weigh a hundred pounds dripping wet. Her naturally dark skin, high cheekbones and sultry eyes spoke of her Pacific Islander heritage versus the effects of continued exposure to the sun.

Another employee, a tall, willowy woman with light brown, wavy hair and startlingly blue eyes Angel recognized as the resort manager, Kiana Williams, stepped out behind her. Trailing the two women was a man dressed in a business suit.

"Mr. Brentwood." The resort manager stopped and placed a hand on the man's chest. "She's not interested in selling."

"Leilani," Brentwood brushed the woman's hand aside and stepped around her to the shorter woman, "they're offering a lot of money. If you accept the offer, you won't have to go through the hassle of cleanup and rebuilding. You can buy a boat, travel the world, move to the mainland or retire and not work another day in your life. At least think about it."

The petite, dark-haired woman turned to face the man, a frown pulling her brows low on her forehead. "I have thought about it every time you bring it up.

My decision stands." She lifted her chin. "No. I won't sell. That land has been in my family for as long as I can remember. Maui is my home, the home of my people, not some faceless corporation that will build high-rises and golf courses, changing everything about this island. It would break my heart if Lahaina became another Honolulu. Now, leave me alone. I have work to do." She laughed. "Me, retired? I'd go out of my mind."

"It will take years to rebuild what was lost," the man named Brentwood said.

Kiana stepped between Brentwood and Leilani. "You heard her. She's not interested, and you're wasting her time." She crossed her arms over her chest. "Now, leave before I have you escorted off the property."

Brentwood frowned heavily. "You can't stop progress."

"Maybe not," Leilani said, "but it won't be at the expense of my heritage."

Brentwood's lips pressed together. "This isn't over," he said. "My clients don't give up easily."

"And I don't like to repeat myself," the resort manager said.

Angel stepped forward, ready to offer to escort Brentwood off the premises. Before he could say anything, the resort manager pulled the radio off her belt and raised it to her lips. "Security, I need two men out front, now."

"I'm going," Brentwood muttered. "But I'm not done."

"Yes. You. Are," Leilani said with a tight smile and turned her attention to Angel, his team and the people milling around the bus. She counted all of them, her full, lush lips moving silently as she tallied the numbers.

While Leilani made a big show of checking her clipboard, Brentwood climbed into a shiny black BMW sports car and spun out of the parking lot, fishtailing like a teenager.

As soon as he was out of sight, the tension seemed to leave Leilani.

"Are you all here for the Waterfall Tour?" Leilani finally asked, projecting her voice to include the elderly tourists near the bus.

Everyone either acknowledged with a nod or an affirming *yes*.

She smiled, the gesture brightening her face, the sunshine glinting off her dark pupils. "I'm your tour guide, Leilani Kealoha. After I check you off my list, you're welcome to climb aboard the bus. We'll get rolling as soon as we're all loaded."

Devlin's lips twisted in a smile. "I believe the tour just got more interesting." He stepped forward. "Devlin Mulhaney," he announced.

Leilani placed a check beside his name. "Aloha, Mr. Mulhaney."

"Call me Dev," he said.

She nodded with a smile. "Dev." Her gaze went past him to Angel.

"Angelo Cortez," Angel said.

Her lips twitched. "Do I call you Angelo or Angel to go with your friend Dev?"

"As a matter of fact, he goes by Angel." Reid abandoned the side of the building and joined the rest of the team.

"Thanks." Angel glared at Reid. "She was talking to me."

Leilani cocked a dark brow. "So, what's it to be?"

Angel's lips twisted. "Angel."

"Angel, it is," Leilani said with a grin.

"I'm Reid Bennet," Reid said and backhanded Teller in the gut. "And this is Teller Osgood."

Teller's cheeks reddened. "Nice to meet you, ma'am."

"Oh, please," Leilani said. "Call me Leilani. You can board the bus now." She crossed to the group of seniors. "Aloha, ladies and gentlemen."

"You heard the lady," Devlin said. "We can get on the bus."

"I'll wait until the others board first," Angel said.

The four men stood back as their guide checked off each name, smiling as she did so.

"I'll be glad when we get to the Big Island," Teller said. "It'll be good to see the rest of the team."

Devlin frowned, "The others are probably living it up on Oahu. There's a lot more to do there. The nightlife is a lot livelier than any other island, and they're right smack in the middle of it on Waikiki Beach. Lucky bastards."

Rex Johnson, Levi Evans, Jackson Jones, Gabe Atkins and Cord Mendez were the other members of their crew of special forces guys who'd formed a black ops team for hire after they'd left their respective branches of the military. They'd worked for a couple of years in various locations from Afghanistan to Syria and, more recently, in Africa.

They might still have been in Africa if Hank Patterson hadn't flown out to meet with them. In his own, very persuasive way, he'd talked them into coming back to the States to man the Hawaii division of the Brotherhood Protectors with the first of his guys to land there, Jace Hawkins, aka Hawk.

Angel had been on a mission with Hawk years ago in Afghanistan. The man had saved his life when a Taliban rebel had thrown a grenade at them.

When the grenade had rolled to a stop at their feet, Hawk had bent, grabbed the grenade and tossed it back in the direction from which it had come. As soon as it had left his hand, he'd tackled Angel, knocking him backward. They'd landed around the corner of a building just as the grenade exploded.

Hawk and Angel had suffered minor and temporary hearing loss. The man who'd thrown the grenade hadn't been as lucky.

Angel owed his life to Hawk and his quick thinking. If the grenade had had a shorter fuse, neither one of them would have survived.

When Hank had mentioned Hawk would be in charge, Angel was sold. Besides, he was tired of the desert and Africa. They all were. The timing couldn't have worked out better. The man funding their work had ended up having a heart attack. The guy who'd taken over wasn't interested in paying them the money promised by his predecessor.

They'd packed their equipment and flown back to the States with Hank, landing in Montana where they'd stayed two nights at Hank's place with his movie star wife, Sadie McClain, and their two kids before being flown to Hawaii for what Hank had insisted was a much-needed vacation.

After two days hanging out at the pool, they'd all grown restless. They'd been running high-octane operations for so long that none of them knew how to power down.

Angel had signed them up for the tour, hoping a little hiking would help burn some energy. If that didn't do it, he'd contact Hawk and ask to come on board earlier than the week they'd been "given" at the resort.

The older tour group members finally made it onto the bus and settled in the seats closest to the front.

Leilani turned to the four men. "Ready?"

Dev grinned. "Ready and willing."

Angel elbowed the man. "Dial back a little. You wreak of desperation."

"I can't help myself." Dev smiled broadly at Leilani before murmuring beneath his breath. "Our guide is hot."

Angel stepped past the man and climbed the steps up onto the bus.

Dev followed, still grinning.

Reid settled in the seat behind Angel and Dev. "She's probably married with half a dozen curtain climbers." He snorted. "But wait. That never stopped you before."

Dev's brow dipped low. "How was I to know Mandy was married? She didn't tell me. I didn't find out until her husband showed up at my apartment, threatening to blow my balls off. I don't make a habit of poaching on another man's woman."

"Mandy?" Reid chuckled. "I was talking about CeCe. The chick in San Diego."

"She said she had broken up with her boyfriend," Dev argued. "She hadn't. It led to an awkward moment when we both showed up at her place to take her out on a date. Being a gentleman, I bowed out gracefully."

Reid snorted.

"How about Layla in Cyprus?" Teller added, taking the seat beside Reid.

"Ha!" Dev's face lit up. "Layla was single. She truly loved me."

With a straight face, Angel asked, "How many children did she have?"

Dev sighed. "Six."

"*Did* she love you?" Reid asked. "Or did she love the idea of you taking care of her and her six children?"

Dev stared at the back of the seat in front of him. "I wasn't ready to be a father of six."

"Nobody is ready to be a father of six," Angel said. "Thankfully, we only had a week in Cyprus before we moved on to our next job."

Dev pressed a hand to his heart. "Layla was beautiful."

"As was CeCe," Reid pointed out.

"And Mandy with her red hair and freckles." Dev sighed again. "I love women."

"You just haven't met one you can trust," Teller concluded.

"A woman you can trust is like a unicorn," Dev said. "You want to believe they exist, but they don't."

At that moment, Leilani climbed the steps onto the bus, laid her clipboard on the dash and slid into the driver's seat.

Angel could barely see the top of her head. His only reassurance she was actually driving was her reflection in the large mirror hanging from the front windshield.

She smiled up into the mirror. "Welcome to

Windsong Tours. Sit back, relax and enjoy the beauty of Maui."

Her smile was genuine, and her stories about Maui, its history and indigenous people were interesting and delivered with such passion. Angel was captivated from the moment they left the resort, following the Hana Highway.

When they arrived at the Ho'olawa Valley's Twin Falls, Leilani parked the small bus in a gravel parking lot near a fresh fruit stand. She quickly dropped to the ground to assist the older passengers as they descended.

She led the group slowly up a gentle slope, following the Big Ho'olawa Stream for a mile, where she took the right fork in the path. They passed an irrigation ditch and soon arrived at the base of Twin Falls.

"Those who don't wish to hike further can stay here and enjoy the falls or swim in the pool," Leilani said. "If you're up for more of a hike, I'll take you to Caveman Falls."

Everyone opted to follow Leilani back to the left fork, past an irrigation ditch and across a stream. Eventually, the path opened to a shallow cave draped with green vines, the waterfall running over the front of the cave before dropping into a shallow pool.

"You can swim here, but the water is shallow and cold," she said. "You have thirty minutes to enjoy the beauty of the area, explore or just sit on the rocks and commune with nature."

The last word had just left her mouth when a flash of skin and speedo burst past the group. With what could only be described as a sound akin to a Native American war cry, Reid splashed into the pool and performed a righteous belly flop. He turned on his back and floated in the midday sunshine.

Several women in the older crowd pulled blankets from their large tote bags and spread them out on the large boulders surrounding the pool. They settled on the blankets and brought out snacks.

Teller and Dev stripped down to their swim trunks and followed Reid into the water, splashing each other and pushing each other beneath the surface.

Leilani came to stand beside Angel, her gaze on the antics of the men in the pool. "Aren't you going to get in with your friends?"

Angelo debated joining the others and shook his head. "We still have a couple more stops. I don't feel like sitting in my wet swimwear for the next couple of hours as we progress through the rest of your waterfall tour."

She smiled. "I brought dry towels."

"I might reconsider." Her smile was infectious and made his lips twitch upward.

"How often do you lead tour groups here?" he asked.

Her smile faded. "I used to lead these tours a lot during the summers to earn extra spending money when I was in high school and college. After college, I didn't conduct the tours anymore, focusing on other aspects of the business." Her brow furrowed. "Until recently."

Something in her tone made Angel study her closer. "Why recently?"

She continued to stare at the men horsing around in the water, though her gaze didn't appear to be focused on them. "The fires changed everything."

He'd heard about the Maui fires on the news, even from where they'd been in Africa. "Were you in one of the affected areas?"

She nodded. "Lahaina."

From what he'd read, Lahaina had been destroyed and was still closed to the public. "I'm sorry," he said.

"Thank you." She closed her eyes for a moment and drew in a deep breath. "Those of us who lost everything are still homeless and trying to find our way." She gave him a tight smile. "Work helps, mentally and financially. Many of our tour guides left Maui to live with relatives on other islands. I fill in where needed. Today was the waterfall tour; tomorrow, I'll work as a deckhand on a boat tour."

"Before the fire, what did you do? You said you went to college. I assume you worked in whatever field in which you majored?"

Her lips twisted. "I owned an art gallery in Lahaina's old town."

Angel frowned. "Was the land where the gallery had been what Brentwood was trying to get you to sell?"

Leilani sighed. "Ever since Lahaina was leveled, opportunists have swooped in, hoping to buy up the land. With no one living there, it's a blank slate that could be developed into huge resorts that could accommodate so many more visitors than previously imagined. They don't have to worry about moving people out of existing homes because there are none. All they need is to buy the land, and they can get started."

"What about the people who lived there? The businesses that were destroyed? Are they coming back?"

Leilani shrugged. "Most can't afford to rebuild. Not at current construction costs. Land and homes that had been in the same families for generations are gone. The people who lived there could barely afford to pay utilities and feed their families before the fires and probably didn't have enough insurance to cover replacement of those homes and businesses."

"I can't imagine the resorts and hotels continuing to house the displaced persons indefinitely," Angel said softly. "What then?"

Leilani shook her head. "I don't know. I'm taking it one day at a time. But I will find a way to rebuild on the land passed down to me from my grandfather. I refuse to sell to big business. If native Hawaiians sell out, we lose our heritage and our culture. I can't let that happen."

For a long moment, Angel stood with Leilani in silence.

"Is there a way to get to the top of the falls?" he asked.

She nodded. "I'll show you. People like to jump off. Today would be a good day to do that. We've had sufficient rain to make the pool deep enough."

Leilani led Angel around the plunge pool to a trail climbing up the side of the hill.

Angel followed, intrigued by this beautiful, petite woman who was knowledgeable about the island's history, flora and fauna. Her love and passion for her home were evident in the care she took to relate its beauty and stories to visitors.

The ground was moist from either a recent rain or heavy morning dew. At several points along the trail, Angel's feet slipped on damp stones.

A few feet ahead of him, Leilani placed her foot on a moss-covered rock. As she lifted her other foot, the one on the mossy rock slipped out from under her.

She teetered for a moment, then pitched backward.

Angel barely had time to react before she slammed into him, knocking him backward.

CHAPTER 3

IT HAPPENED SO fast Angel only had a split second to react. He caught Leilani in his arms, crushing her back to his chest as he lost his own balance and sat down hard on the trail, teetering precariously close to the edge. After a few scary moments, he was able to steady himself in time to keep them both from tumbling down the hillside.

Leilani lay sprawled across his lap, her head resting against his shoulder, the fragrant scent of her hair wafting up to his nostrils.

He held her around the waist, afraid that if he let go, she'd tumble down the hill, or worse, over the ledge to fall among the rocks and boulders below.

For a long moment, they sat still. The longer he held her, the more he liked how her body felt against his.

"Are you okay?" Leilani asked softly.

"I am," he said, loosening his hold only slightly around her waist. "You?"

She nodded. "That could've been a bad fall for both of us. Thanks."

"You're welcome." Still, he held onto her, liking how warm and soft she was. Having someone this close reminded him of how long it had been since he'd been with a woman.

Too long.

"You can let go now," Leilani said.

"The trail's narrow and damp here," he said. "Are you sure you can stand without slipping over the edge?"

"Yes," she replied.

"I'd feel better if you held onto my hand as you rise."

"Deal," she said.

When he released his hold around her waist, he reached for her hand and held on tightly.

Leilani managed to stand on the trail. She grabbed for a nearby root jutting out of the side of the hill and held on as Angel eased to his feet.

"If it's all right with you," she said, "I'd rather not risk another fall."

He grinned. "Same. We can go back down to where the others are. I'll go first, but please, continue to hold onto me until we reach the bottom."

She hadn't removed her hand from his and didn't, even after they made it to the base of the hill.

Reid lay sprawled across a large boulder, soaking up the sunshine in his navy-blue Speedo swimsuit.

Dev and Teller were emerging from the pool as Angel and Leilani rejoined the group.

Dev's gaze zeroed in on Angel and Leilani's joined hands, and his eyebrows shot up. "Look who got the jump on me." He tipped his head toward them. "Turn my back for a minute, and the Angel gets one step ahead of the Dev." He winked.

Teller stepped up on shore and shook the water from his hands and arms. "Shut up, Dev. It's not like you had a claim."

Leilani pulled her hand free of Angel's and shoved it into the back pocket of her jeans. "If you've all had enough time here at Twin Falls, we should be moving on to our next stop. Let's make our way back to the bus."

She left Angel with the guys and hurried over to help the ladies pack their blankets and snack wrappings.

Reid rolled to his feet, pulled on his khaki pants and boots and dragged his polo shirt over his head. Dev and Teller dressed quickly and shoved their feet into their boots.

Soon, they were on the way back to the bus, moving a little faster going downhill than when they'd ascended the trail.

Angel hung back, not wanting to crowd Leilani. Though he missed holding her hand.

When they arrived at the bus, Leilani stopped short and muttered a curse. "Son of a bitch."

Angel hurried forward. "What's wrong?"

She tipped her chin toward the rear of the bus. "Flat tire."

Angel frowned and bent to inspect the tire. The sidewall had a large slash in the rubber.

Reid walked around the other side of the bus and called out, "It's not the only flat tire. Two more on this side."

"I only have one spare." Leilani pulled her cell phone out of her back pocket.

Angel pulled out his cell phone at the same time, glad to note it hadn't been broken in their fall and that it had reception.

Leilani scrolled through her contacts, selected one and placed her call. "Hey, I could use some help. I have a group of ten plus me at Twin Falls—no engine trouble...flat tires. You heard me right. Three out of four. Slashed. We'll be here waiting for rescue. Thanks."

After she ended the call, she glanced around at her tour group.

Angel wished he could do more to help the situation, but he suspected Leilani had everything under control.

"I'm sorry to inform you that we will not be able to continue our waterfall tour due to multiple flat tires," Leilani said. "I have help on the way, but if you'd like to take a seat in the bus, you're more than welcome, and I can run the air conditioner."

The older members of the group filed into the crippled bus and sat in the seats.

Angel and his teammates gathered around Leilani.

"Someone slashed those tires," Reid said.

"Any idea who might have done it?" Angel asked.

Leilani shook her head, her brow creased. "No, and this isn't the first incident like this."

Angel reached for her hand. "What else has happened?"

Her fingers curled around his. "Someone tampered with one of our tour boats."

"In what way?" Angel asked.

"They filled it with diesel," she said.

"That could happen to anyone not paying attention at the pump," Angel countered.

Leilani nodded. "The only thing is there's no credit card record of the boat being refueled. My guys use the company credit card every time. They don't pull that kind of money out of their pockets. And the boats don't come out of the water often, only when they're drydocked for maintenance. Diesel pumps aren't anywhere near where my guys fuel up. Someone had to bring the diesel to the boat and pour it in."

"Your guys?" Dev's eyebrow cocked. "You're not just a tour guide?"

Leilani shook her head. "No. I'm the lucky owner

trying to keep my business afloat until we can return to some sense of normal."

"Color me impressed," Dev said. "I admire strong, smart women."

"Because you're a wimpy dumbass," Reid quipped.

Angel ignored his teammates' banter, more concerned about this woman's troubles. "Any other issues?"

She nodded. "I might've counted the diesel off as an employee mistake, but one of the rails on the boat had been cut almost all the way through. When my boat captain leaned against it, the rail snapped, and he fell overboard."

"Damn." Angel squeezed her fingers gently. "Is he okay?"

"Fortunately, he wasn't injured, but the boat has been out of commission for a couple of days to drain the tank, change the spark plugs and repair or replace the damaged rail. That's several days of canceled tours, and that crew has been out of work." She sighed. "Today's event will be another hit to Windsong Tours when I refund money because we couldn't complete the entire tour. As it was, we were going to be tight on making payments on the new bus we had to buy when the old one burned in the fire."

"Didn't your insurance cover the bus?" Reid asked.

Leilani laughed. "They covered the current value

of the older model bus, not the replacement value of getting a new one. Without the income from the storefront businesses we had on Front Street in Lahaina, our only sources of income are the land and sea tours—and we were just starting to get reservations as tourists return to Maui."

"Why would someone want to sabotage your business?" Teller asked.

Leilani raised her hands, palms up. "I don't know."

"A scorned lover?" Dev offered.

Angel shot him a narrow-eyed glance.

"What? It could happen," Dev said. "I had an old girlfriend key my truck. Slashed tires aren't that different."

Leilani chuckled. "No old boyfriends. I haven't been on a date in over a year. Between the businesses, the fires and recovery..." She shook her head.

Interesting. She hadn't been on a date in a year? Angel's immediate thought was that he wanted to be the man to break that streak. But first, they needed to figure out who was targeting her and her business. "Competitors?" Angel suggested.

"I've never had trouble with our competitors in the past. We share information about weather and oceanic conditions. When we're booked solid, we refer customers to each other."

"When did the troubles start?" Angel asked.

"Shortly after they reopened Maui for tourism again."

"Your competition could be hungry enough to want all the tours," Teller said.

She gave them a weak smile. "We're all trying to work to put food on the table. The free meals many of the restaurants, resorts and local farms are providing can't last forever."

"True," Angel agreed.

Leilani continued, "The lack of housing is a huge problem. Many of the people from Lahaina who worked in the service industry have left the island. Those who remain are being housed in the resorts and vacation rentals."

Angel nodded. "And as the number of tourists increases, they'll have to find alternative housing options."

She nodded. "Right. And that includes me. I'm staying at the same resort as you. I have nowhere else to go."

"No family elsewhere on the island?" Reid asked.

She shook her head. "Nor on any other island. My folks passed during the COVID pandemic. It's just me and my cousin Makai. He's staying at one of the other resorts. He's in the same position as so many others. The homes we lived in are gone, along with all our possessions."

"Is your cousin part of your family business?" Angel asked.

Leilani shook her head. "No. That's a long story in itself."

Reid crossed his arms over his chest. "We have nothing better to do until your help arrives."

Angel nodded. "He's right. If you don't mind sharing, we're listening."

Leilani drew in a deep breath and let it out. "Before my grandfather passed away, he asked his two sons what parts of the family business they wanted to inherit. I think my grandfather knew that my father and uncle didn't see eye to eye on many things. He wanted to leave something to each of his sons but didn't want them to argue over how to run things."

"Your grandfather sounds like he was a smart man," Angel said.

Leilani looked down at her hands. "He was. He set up his will so that they got equal assets. When my grandfather passed, the oldest son, my uncle, got the apartment complex my grandfather owned in Lahaina. My father got the strip of stores on Front Street my grandfather inherited from his father." She looked away. "My grandfather had just finished a major remodel on the apartments and its exterior. My uncle didn't waste much time before he sold the apartment complex and moved to Vegas."

"Did your cousin go with his father?" Angel asked.

Leilani shook her head. "Makai didn't want to leave Maui. He loved the life here, and surfing is his passion. When my uncle left, my father offered to take my cousin into our home and put him to work in the family business."

"That was good of your father to offer," Angel said.

Leilani smiled. "My father was a good man. He loved his brother, even when he disagreed with his decisions. He loved Lahaina, the people, our culture. He would do anything to help others. He didn't mind helping people out who were in a tight fix, but he also expected able-bodied people to help themselves."

"And your cousin wanted a handout but didn't want to work for it?" Teller asked.

"Sort of," Leilani's brow twisted. "Dad had just started to renovate the stores, using some of the money he'd inherited along with the buildings. He used the rest as a down payment on boats to diversify from being strictly a shop owner to being a tour company owner. Makai didn't like the idea of starting at the bottom as a construction helper or deckhand and working his way up. He felt that, as family, he should have elevated status in the company, like manager over the tour company or one of the shops. Makai declined my father's offer and went to work for one of the resorts." She gave them a half smile. "Sorry. You didn't ask for our complete family history."

Angel smiled. "No, I'm glad you're willing to share."

"Makai's father didn't leave him anything before moving to Vegas?" Dev asked.

Leilani shook her head. "Makai and Uncle Jim had a falling out the day before my uncle and his wife left. As far as I know, they never spoke again to each other."

"Are your uncle and his wife still living in Vegas?" Reid asked.

"No. Uncle Jim and Aunt Rita died in a helicopter crash over the Grand Canyon a couple of years after he sold the apartments. I left college to attend the funeral with my father. Makai didn't come. I found out later he'd gone surfing instead."

"Did Makai inherit the apartment money from his father?" Angel asked, suspecting he already knew the answer.

"No." Leilani's lips pressed together. "Uncle Jim had purchased an expensive home in Vegas and blew through what money was left over, remodeling that house and gambling. When he ran out of cash, he accrued a massive amount of credit card debt. It took the sale of his house to repay most of his debt. As far as I know, it wasn't enough. Makai got nothing but the mess his father left."

Angel frowned. "Could he be resentful of what you have?"

She shrugged. "Maybe. I reached out to him after the fire to see if I could help him in any way I could. He said he didn't need my help, that the resort where he worked had taken in their employees who'd lost their homes. He expected the resort to reopen soon. They were one of the first to start taking tourists after they opened Maui up to visitors."

"To me, it sounds like your cousin could be a prime suspect."

"Why would he want my business to fail?" Leilani shook her head. "What's in it for him?"

"Misery loves company?" Dev said.

Leilani's lips twisted. "Seems like a lot of work to make someone else miserable. Especially when we're all trying to figure out life without Lahaina. Besides, he and his fiancée, Alyssa, are doing well enough, as far as I can tell. She's a competitive surfer like Makai. That's how they met. Their wedding was put on hold after the fire, but they've since set another date. It's full steam ahead on the planning. Alyssa even asked me to be one of her bridesmaids. I can't imagine Makai would be at the bottom of my business's sabotage."

"Other than family drama and competitors, are there any others who might want your business to fail?" Angel asked. "I read some Maui residents don't want the tourists back."

"There's truth in that statement," Leilani said. "Some locals would be just as happy if tourists didn't return. When they arrive in massive numbers, they disturb the ecological systems, and some of them disrespect cultural boundaries and ignore no trespassing signs."

Angel could understand residents being resentful of strangers desecrating sacred grounds. "Do these locals have anyone in particular leading the charge?"

"Buddy Akina has been pretty loud lately, campaigning against tourism," Leilani said. "He's put his hat in the ring to run for state senator. Our state governor has shut him down a couple of times recently, though, to placate Buddy, she promised a phased approach to reopening Maui so as not to overwhelm the Maui residents who are still grieving the losses of loved ones and homes."

"What about the man you were arguing with as you left the resort earlier?" Angel asked. "Brentwood someone?"

Leilani gave a short bark of laughter. "Pete Brentwood is annoying, but he's harmless. He's only one of a number of brokers who've been stalking Lahaina landowners, hoping to buy cheap property while it's nothing but rubble."

"If they're determined to get you to sell, they could sabotage your business," Angel said. "You said yourself that you need the money from tours to make payments on the boats and fund your employees' salaries. If they keep you from providing those tours..."

"I won't have the funds to keep operations running." Leilani crossed her arms over her chest. "I'll just have to be more vigilant and do my best to stay ahead of the attacks."

"You can't be everywhere or watch all your assets twenty-four-seven," Angel pointed out. "You're only one person."

Dev grinned. "Maybe we can help. At least, while we're here for the rest of the week."

Leilani's brow twisted. "I can't afford to pay my employees. How do you expect me to pay all of you?" She shook her head. "No, I can't ask you to give up your vacation to help me."

"You didn't ask," Angel looked at his teammates. "We're offering to do it free of charge. Right, guys?"

"Right," they agreed in unison.

Angel grinned. "I noticed a signup board for guests to volunteer at local businesses as a way to give back to the people of Maui. This will be our contribution."

"I can hang out with the bus to make sure no one slashes its tires," Teller said. "Where do you park it when it's not in use?"

"In the resort parking lot," Leilani said. "They have cameras, so I don't think it'd be necessary to monitor it overnight. We could always tap into the surveillance videos if it happens on the resort property. It's when we take guests out that it's most vulnerable, and our guests are left stranded."

"I'll go with the bus, then," Teller said. "When's the next tour?"

"Tomorrow," Leilani said. "My assistant, Olina, is scheduled to lead the tour as long as her babysitter doesn't bail."

Reid held up both hands. "Sorry, I'll volunteer to cook, clean, swab decks or ride along with tour groups, but I draw the line at childcare. I'm not good with little people."

Leilani grinned. "Even if you were, Olina would hesitate to leave her kids with a stranger. She's got one of the other Lahaina refugees lined up to keep an eye on her children after they get out of school."

"Where else do you need enhanced security?" Angel asked.

"We have two snorkeling tours scheduled for tomorrow. One of my captains is picking up the repaired boat as we speak. He volunteered to sleep on it tonight to make sure no one comes back to trash it again. My other captain has been alternating with his deckhands to stand guard on the other boat at night. They could use some relief if any of you are up to roughing it on a craft that's not designed to be lived on."

"Now, you're talking," Reid said. "I can take the night shift on one."

"I'll take night shift on the other," Dev volunteered. "And, if it's okay, I'll hang with the crew when they go out tomorrow."

"Since the night shift is covered," Angel said, "I'd like to ride with the other boat."

Leilani's cheeks reddened. "I'd like that. I'm working as a deckhand on the boat returning from the marina's maintenance shop. I like to see for myself that it's running properly." Her gaze met his, making him warm inside.

Angel had to remind himself not to get too attached. They were only on Maui for the rest of the week. Then, they'd have to report to the Big Island to start work with the Brotherhood Protectors.

In the meantime, it wouldn't hurt to get to know more about Maui and its intrepid inhabitants, namely one fierce but petite business owner.

CHAPTER 4

THE RUSH of heat filling Leilani's cheeks surprised her. She hadn't been this affected by a man in...well...ever.

Sure, she'd dated in high school and college, and she'd had lovers, but this felt different. So different, she found herself agreeing to allow these men to help her guard what was left of her tour fleet.

Had she lost her mind? She'd only just met the four guys. What did she know about them?

Not a damned thing.

Angel must have sensed her hesitation. "Just so you know, we're not serial killers or spies sent over from big corporations to undermine your recovery efforts." He looked around at his teammates. "I've served with these men on active duty or when we hired out as contract mercenaries. These guys are good men with the strongest code of ethics. But how do I convince you when you know nothing about any of them?"

"Don't take his word for it," Reid said. "Google an organization called the Brotherhood Protectors. You'll find the name Hank Patterson. Navy SEAL. You might have heard of his wife, Sadie McClain?"

Leilani frowned. "That name sounds familiar. Sadie McClain..."

Dev laughed. "She's only the highest-paid megastar actor in Hollywood."

"But that's beside the point," Angel said. "Do like Reid says, google Hank, find the phone number for Brotherhood Protectors. Call. Not only will Hank answer the call, but he'll vouch for us."

"So?" Leilani challenged. "I call a stranger to vouch for four more strangers?" She laughed. "No. I must be getting desperate even to consider letting you help me."

"Just call Hank," Teller said. "He'll know how to convince you that we're on the up and up."

"That's right," Angel agreed. "We're all prior military special operations." He pointed to Reid. "Tell her."

"Navy SEAL," Reid said.

Dev raised a hand. "Marine Force Recon. Hoo-ah!"

Teller lifted his chin. "Delta Force."

When Leilani looked at Angel, he stood taller. "Navy SEAL."

Her frown deepened. "My gut tells me to trust you."

"Don't," Angel said. "Do the due diligence. Look us up. We want you to feel confident that we have your back."

"More importantly," Reid added, "that we are capable of protecting you."

"I'll do that," she said. "In the meantime, our backup transportation has arrived."

While they'd been talking, the hotel shuttle had arrived, pulling to a stop near the disabled tour bus. A large tow truck arrived seconds behind the shuttle. The guests waiting patiently inside the bus disembarked and transferred to the resort shuttle. As soon as the bus was empty, the men in the tow truck quickly secured it for transport.

The tow truck driver met with Leilani and handed her a business card. "Your bus will be at our shop. If we have the right-sized tires, our guys can replace them before the day's end. Call before you come to make sure we have the tires."

"I will," Leilani said. "And if all goes well, I'll have someone swing by to pick up the bus before you close for the day. I really need it for tomorrow."

Angel stood silently by her side throughout the exchange. He didn't try to take over or show off any manly ability to talk auto shop with the tow truck driver.

Leilani found Angel refreshing. Because Leilani

was short, men often treated her as though she were a child, not a savvy businesswoman with a good, if basic understanding of tires, mechanics and fair prices on both. In most cases, once men realized she wasn't a pushover, they gave their observations to her straight. No embellishments or talking down to her.

The tow truck driver waved to Leilani as he drove out of the gravel parking lot.

Leilani climbed the steps into the resort shuttle and smiled at the faces turned in her direction. "Thank you all for your patience. We should arrive back at the resort in half an hour. And, since we were unable to complete the day's itinerary, Windsong Tours will refund your money."

"Ms. Leilani." An elderly gentleman raised a hand as if he were still in elementary school.

"Yes, sir." Leilani smiled gently, grateful the guests were getting along well enough they didn't mind being cooped up on a bus for a while.

"Some of us discussed what we paid for the tour and agreed we got our money's worth at Twin Falls. A refund is unnecessary. We know you, your family and your employees lost a lot in the fire. We didn't want to make matters worse by demanding our money back. It's our gift to you and your employees."

"Hear! Hear!" shouted the younger men in the back of the bus.

Leilani's chest swelled, and her eyes burned.

"Thank you all so very much." Their gesture was so generous her heart swelled.

For the journey back to the resort, she shared more of the history of Maui and the chain of Hawaiian Islands and some of their customs passed down through the generations.

Time seemed to pass quickly. Before she realized it, they were pulling into the parking lot at the resort.

As the guests exited the shuttle, each person handed her a tip and thanked her for taking them to the falls and for all the stories.

In turn, Leilani thanked them for their generosity and reminded them of the snorkeling tours offered the following day.

Angel was the last guest to leave the resort shuttle. He took his time coming down the steps and stopped for a long moment in front of her. When he handed her a twenty-dollar bill, she held up her hands. "That's too much."

"Then give it to someone you know who needs it." He folded her hand around the bill, his fingers cupping hers. "I'm sure you know plenty who do."

"I do," she said, thinking of people living in the resort who only had the items donated through churches, the Red Cross and private donors. Most were unemployed, the jobs they'd had having gone up in flames with the buildings of Lahaina. "That's where all my tips go," she murmured.

Leilani was one of the lucky survivors of the fires.

Not only did she make it out alive, but parts of her businesses were still operational, generating income as soon as Maui had reopened to tourists. Thanks to her captains, two of her three boats had been moved out of the harbor before the fire reached them.

Angel pulled a business card from his wallet and handed it to Leilani. "Let me know what you decide about my team helping you out. We won't do anything until you give us the go-ahead."

She stared down at the card, reading the words Brotherhood Protectors in bold letters and his name, Angelo Cortez. "A business card makes your service sound legit."

He chuckled. "Anyone can print a business card. Not everyone has the training or experience we have. Call Hank. I'll wait to hear from you."

She looked up from the card and smiled. "Thanks. I'll do that as soon as I get back to my room."

"Good." He gave her a brief nod. "Thanks again for an inspiring tour."

She snorted. "What little we were able to accomplish."

"It was enough...for now. I'll see you later," he said and left her standing beside the shuttle. When the driver closed the door and drove away, Leilani walked across the sprawling grounds to the section of the resort designated for the refugees from the Lahaina fire.

Tucked away from the rest of the structures, this

area had a more lived-in appearance. Small children played on the lush green grass while the adults sat nearby. Some visited with their neighbors, others hung laundry on makeshift clotheslines or stared off into space. Though the fire was in the past, the memories and grief were still fresh, raw and real.

Leilani waved at a few of the women as she passed and entered the room she'd been assigned. Thankfully, it had a bedroom, a sitting area and a kitchenette where she could prepare food for herself. The resort kitchens and local restaurants provided free meals to people who'd lost their homes in the fires, but Leilani preferred to make her breakfast and soups and salad.

She made a beeline for her new laptop, thankful all over again that she'd stored everything to do with her business in the cloud. She'd been able to access all her data once she'd received the laptop and logged in.

Following Angelo's advice, she performed a search on the internet for the Brotherhood Protectors and found several references and phone numbers for offices in Eagle Rock, Montana; Fool's Gold, Colorado; West Yellowstone, Montana; Bayou Mambaloa, Louisiana; and the Big Island of Hawaii. Apparently, business was good for the organization to spread across the nation.

As suggested, she looked for Hank Patterson and found several articles about the former Navy SEAL who'd opened a security agency providing protective services to anyone who needed them. Several news articles referenced Hank and the Brotherhood Protectors for their successes in stopping an organization from overthrowing the government, shutting down a sex trafficking ring in Wyoming and protecting a U.S. Congresswoman during her election campaign.

She found the phone number for the Brotherhood Protectors in Eagle Rock, Montana, and punched the numbers into her cell phone. For a moment, she hesitated. Was it necessary to actually call the man? From what she'd found, she could easily assume Brotherhood Protectors was a legitimate organization.

That didn't mean the four men who were staying at the resort actually worked for the Brotherhood Protectors.

She hit the call button.

A man's voice answered on the first ring. "Brotherhood Protectors, Hank Patterson speaking."

Stunned that the head of the organization answered, Leilani couldn't form words.

The man chuckled. "I see from the caller ID that this call originates in Hawaii. Is this Leilani Kealoha?"

"Uh. Yes, it is," she said, pulling herself together. "And you're Hank Patterson, the owner and founder of Brotherhood Protectors?"

"Yes, ma'am," he responded. "I just got off the phone with one of my guys, Angelo Cortez. He said to expect a call from you. He wanted me to reassure you that he works for the Brotherhood. And he does. Granted, he and his team are new to the organization, but I served with Angelo and Reid Bennet in the Navy. They're good men."

"That's nice to know," Leilani said.

"Still not convinced we are who we say we are?" Hank asked. "I get it. It's hard to trust anyone over a telephone call; you can't see the truth in their eyes or read their body language. Look, can I switch us over to a video call?"

"Uh," Leilani frowned, "I guess that will be fine." She wasn't sure why that would make a difference, but whatever.

Her cell phone rang with an incoming video call. When she answered, a man's face appeared. He had dark hair, green eyes and a friendly smile.

"That's better," he said. "Nice to meet you, Ms. Kealoha."

"Mr. Patterson," she acknowledged.

"Hank?" a female voice called out in the background on Hank's side.

Hank turned. "In here," he responded and grinned at Leilani. "Sorry. My home is my office. The boss is calling." He turned as a woman appeared on the screen, carrying a baby.

She had a long blond ponytail and no makeup on her face, but she was beautiful nonetheless.

Leilani recognized her immediately, and her heart skipped several beats. "You're Sadie McClain."

The woman smiled. "I am." She glanced down at the baby on her hip. "This is McClain, and he needs his diaper changed."

"And it's my turn, isn't it?" Hank reached for the baby. "Sadie, this is Leilani Kealoha, a potential client. Talk to her while I fix this little guy up." He stood as he spoke. "I'll be back."

Sadie sank into the seat Hank had vacated. "What do you want to know?"

Leilani shook her head. "I don't know what to ask. I've never spoken to a movie star before."

"Oh, sweetie, let me tell you a secret..." Sadie leaned forward, her eyes narrowing. "You might not believe this, but," she paused and looked over her shoulder as if someone might be eavesdropping, then she said, "we're people, too." Sadie laughed. "So, are you thinking you might hire the Brotherhood Protectors?"

Leilani frowned. "Not exactly. It's not like I have money to pay them for security services."

Sadie waved a hand at the screen. "That's not a problem. Hank and I decided in the beginning to take all clients regardless of their ability to pay. If you need help, we provide it."

Leilani's eyes widened. "Seriously? I thought the guys here just wanted to volunteer while they were on vacation."

"And that might be so." Sadie folded her hands on the desk in front of her. "You're on Maui, right?"

Leilani nodded.

"I read that tourists who were vacationing on Maui are volunteering as a way to help the people of Maui recover from the fires."

"That's true," Leilani agreed. "So many people are homeless and unemployed."

"I'm so sorry for what happened," Sadie said. "I take it you're one of those displaced people?"

Leilani nodded.

"And now, you're having troubles and need a little help. That makes it even worse. You don't know who to trust. And these strangers appear and offer to provide that help free of charge."

"That sums it up," Leilani said.

"From what Hank told me, the guys volunteered to help. I'm not surprised. The men Hank hires for the Brotherhood Protectors aren't used to lying around the pool, drinking Mai Tais. At least not for long. They're used to high-octane, heart-racing operations that challenge them physically and mentally. They've been there two, maybe three days, and are probably bored out of their minds. They're good men. Hank wouldn't hire them if they weren't. And they have skills most civilians can only imagine. If they have your back, you're in good hands."

Hank reappeared with a giggling baby. "I'm back."

Sadie smiled. "I enjoyed talking with you, Leilani. Maybe someday soon, I can talk my husband into taking me to Hawaii. If we come, I'd love to meet you in person."

"I'd like that," Leilani said, completely at ease with the famous movie star, who was amazingly down-to-earth and pleasant.

Sadie slipped out of the chair and reached for the baby.

The child tucked his arms in and buried his face against Hank's neck.

"Traitor," Sadie muttered.

"He's okay where he is," Hank said. "Did you convince Ms. Kealoha we're trustworthy and the guys I've sent her way are the real deal?"

Sadie turned to Leilani with her beautiful brow cocked. "Did I?"

Leilani laughed. "You did. Thank you for spending the time with me."

"Good. Hank's one of the good guys, as are the people he hires." She dropped a kiss on her husband's head. "I'm going to check on Emma. Don't forget you have kitchen duty tonight." She winked at Leilani. "Nice to meet you." Sadie disappeared, leaving Hank and the baby on the screen.

"Told you she was the boss," Hank said. "Are we good? Are you more comfortable with the idea of letting my guys help?"

Leilani nodded. "I feel much better."

"Those guys are four of the ten men I sent to Hawaii to man the Hawaiian branch of the Brotherhood Protectors. They might be new to this organization, but they're all experienced in defense, extraction and protection. They'll take care of you and help you figure out who's behind your troubles."

The baby in Hank's arms smashed his face against Hank's and blew loud, wet raspberries.

Hank's lips twisted. "Anytime you need me, just call. Now, if we're done here, I have steaks to grill and a salad to chop. Nice to meet you."

"Nice to meet you, Mr. Patterson," Leilani said.

"Call me Hank," he corrected. "Out here." The call ended.

Leilani stared at the black screen, a smile on her face. Hank and Sadie seemed to be super nice, and the news reports she'd found had spoken highly of the Brotherhood Protectors' work.

The men hadn't asked for money. So, why was she hesitant to call Angel and let him know she was on board with them helping her?

Could it be that because, if they were helping her, she'd be around Angel a lot more? Just the few hours she'd been with him had made her feel things she hadn't felt for a man in a long time. He made her tingly all over. When she'd fallen into his lap, she hadn't wanted to get up. She hadn't wanted him to stop holding her. The strength of that desire to be held had almost been too much.

And to be around him all day would be a challenge she wasn't sure she could handle. Especially after months of grief, of not knowing whether she had a viable business, no clue as to when she would have a home again or when they would be allowed to return to Lahaina to start the rebuilding process.

Leilani was not at a good place in her life for the complication of a relationship.

Not that Angel was signing up for that job.

Why was she getting all worked up about working with the man?

She entered his number into her contact list with his name, Angelo Cortez. After all, he was going to work with her for the next few days.

Then, he'd move on to his new job with the Brotherhood Protectors based on the Big Island. Not that far away, but definitely out of range of hopping into a car and driving over to pick her up for a date.

Again...he wasn't signing up for the job of dating her.

Leilani shook herself and called his number before she could talk herself out of it again.

He answered on the first ring. "This is Angel."

Her face heated, and her tongue refused to work immediately. "Hey," she managed to get out.

"Leilani?" he asked, his tone deep and warm, spreading over her like the heated water of a tidal pool, seeping into every pore of her body.

"It's me," she said. "I wanted to let you know I just got off a video call with Hank." She smiled as she remembered the conversation with the couple from Montana. "And Sadie McClain."

Angel chuckled. "They're an amazing team. What did you think about them?"

"I liked them immediately. I also researched Brotherhood Protectors on the internet. They've done some good things."

"So? Are you going to let us help you?" he asked.

Leilani nodded, even though Angel couldn't see her. "Yes."

"Great! I'll let the guys know they're on tonight and tomorrow."

"Thank you," Leilani said.

"But before I call them," Angel said. "I wanted to ask you a question."

"Go ahead, but I warn you," she laughed, "I might not know the answer."

"It's a simple question requiring only a yes or no."

"Good," she braced herself for his query.

"Will you have dinner with me tonight?" Angel asked.

Leilani hadn't expected that kind of question.

"I—" she swallowed hard.

"We'll need to go over the details of the assignment," he added quickly.

"Oh, yes. Of course." Her cheeks flamed. Leilani was glad he couldn't see her embarrassment. "Although, dinner isn't necessary. We could meet in the lobby."

"I'll be hungry, and it would kill two birds with one stone," he persisted. "Of course, if you're uncomfortable having dinner with me, I completely understand."

"No. No," she hurried to say. "Dinner will be fine. I can meet you in one of the resort's restaurants."

He suggested the name of the steak and lobster restaurant on the resort. "Six o'clock?"

"I'll see you at six," she said. "In the meantime, I'll let my boat captains know your men will take the night shift at ten and give them a break."

"Calling my guys now," he said. "See you soon."

Leilani ended the call and immediately called her boat captains, letting them know she'd "hired" help to guard the boats overnight, giving them Reid and Dev's names. After agreeing on the time they should meet at the marina, she ended the last call and stared at her cell phone.

She was going to dinner with a man. "At the most exclusive restaurant on the resort." She frowned. "I have nothing to wear."

Literally.

She had nothing that fancy to wear. A glance at the time made her heart kick into overdrive. She had only a couple of hours to find something to wear, shower, do her hair and be there.

"Shoot!" Leilani shot to her feet and ran for the small closet, knowing nothing in it would suffice. She looked around the room, at a loss. Where could she get a dress on such short notice?

Her cell phone rang on the table where she'd left it.

She started to ignore it, then hurried to answer. If it was Angel, she'd tell him she couldn't meet him for dinner.

The caller ID showed Kiana Williams, her friend and the resort manager.

Leilani answered. "Kiana, thank God."

The other woman chuckled. "No one's ever thanked God for me, but, hey, I'll take it. I have a broker here who insists on speaking with you. Want me to tell him to take a hike?"

"Please," Leilani said. "But call me back. I have an emergency you might be able to help me with."

"Now, I'm intrigued," she said. "I'll be right back." Her friend ended the call.

Leilani held the cell phone in front of her, willing it to ring again, praying Kiana could help her.

The cell phone barely rang when Leilani answered the call from Kiana.

"So, what's your emergency?" Kiana asked. "Did a broker make it past security? Is one of our guests stalking you? Did a gecko take up residence in your suite?"

"No." Leilani laughed. "It's worse. I need a dress for dinner tonight."

"A what?" Kiana asked.

"A dress." Leilani sighed. "You remember the guys who went on the tour with me today?"

"The ones with the silver hair or the hot ones that could make a girl's panties damp?"

"The hot ones," Leilani said.

"Don't tell me you have a date with all four of them," Kiana said. "That's just bragging and selfish if you ask me."

"No. Just one." Leilani drew in a deep breath to steady her breathing and slow her pulse. "He wants me to join him at the Kea Hana Restaurant."

"Sweet," Kiana said. "The man's making an effort to impress."

"We're talking business," Leilani said.

"Uh-huh." Kiana chuckled. "What kind of business?"

"Pull your mind out of the gutter, girl," Leilani shook her head, a smile tugging at her lips. Trust Kiana to think about sex. She hadn't been on a date since taking the job as resort manager. Like Leilani, she'd been focused on the job, not her sex life. "His team is going to provide security for my tour business for the week. We're going to go over the details."

"Over steak and lobster?" Kiana clucked her tongue. "He's not just talking business. The man's into you. And why not? You're one hot hoochie mama when you're not wearing the company polo shirt."

"That's just it," Leilani held the phone tightly. "I

don't have anything fancy enough to wear to the Kea Hana, and I don't have time to go shopping. Help!"

"Oh, sweetie, that's right. I doubt seriously the donations included cocktail dresses. But you know, I might be able to help you."

"Oh, thank God," Leilani sank into a chair. "Surely, you have a dress I could borrow."

"Actually," Kiana dragged out the word, "I doubt any of my dresses would fit you. I'm a couple sizes larger than you and almost a foot taller."

Leilani sighed. "It sucks to be short."

"It sucks being tall, except when you have to go toe-to-toe in an argument with a man." Kiana chuckled. "But don't worry. I think we can find something in our lost and found room. You'd be surprised with the things guests leave behind. Come up to the lodge. I'll show you."

"Do you have time? I don't want to take you away from your work," Leilani said.

"I always have time for emergencies," Kiana said. "And a date qualifies—especially after a long dry spell."

"It's not a date," Leilani insisted as she hurried out the door of her suite.

"Keep telling yourself that," Kiana's voice dripped with sarcasm. "You might believe it. I don't."

Minutes later, after practically running across the sprawling resort, Leilani stood in the far corner of a large storage room full of supplies. Clothes hung on several racks pushed up against the back wall, along with half a dozen large boxes filled with clothes, beach toys, hats and sunglasses.

Kiana stood with her arms crossed over her chest, shaking her head. "I should've thought about it sooner. I'm sure there are things all of our Lahaina guests could use. I'll send out a notice for them to come take a look. But first, let's get you dressed for your date."

"It's not a date," Leilani murmured as she riffled through expensive suits and beautiful dresses guests had forgotten in their hurry to return home from vacation.

Life had become surreal since the fires had destroyed all her belongings. She'd taken pride in her independence and ability to provide for herself. Now, she and so many others relied on handouts to get by. Even if they could afford to pay for things, sometimes, scarcity made it impossible to get them.

Leilani thought she was done crying over all they'd lost in the fire, but she found her eyes welling with tears.

She tried to brush them away before Kiana saw them, but her friend was too observant.

"Hey." Kiana pulled Leilani into her arms. "It's okay. You'll get through this. We'll all get through this."

Leilani leaned into Kiana's arms. For the past months since the fire had destroyed so much, Leilani had put on a brave face with an attitude of "fake it until you feel it."

"I don't know what's wrong with me," she admitted.

"Nothing's wrong with you," Kiana leaned back and brushed the hair from Leilani's face. "I'd think something was wrong with you if you didn't fall apart even a little after all you've been through." She smiled down at her friend. "Now, come on. I believe that if you look good, you feel good. Let's find something that makes you look great."

In the process of losing things, Leilani had gained a better understanding of what was truly important in her life.

People.

CHAPTER 5

ANGEL PACED OUTSIDE the entrance to the Kea Hana Restaurant, tugging at the necktie Reid had helped him tie earlier.

Like the others, Angel had come with everything he owned in a suitcase and a duffle bag. After leaving the military and working as a contract mercenary, he'd learned he didn't need a lot of things. Having an apartment hadn't made sense if he was never home or even in the States for any length of time.

When he'd left the Navy, he'd sold or donated all his furniture and household goods. The clothes he'd kept were just enough to get him to the next laundry facility.

The suit was new. He figured he might need one in case he had to provide security for a wealthy client. Reid had been the one to suggest that they invest in a suit, nice trousers and a couple of classy shirts. He'd even helped the guys shop for them in Oahu before they'd taken the hop to Maui.

Though the suit fit him perfectly, it was still a suit. Angel was most comfortable in a T-shirt, cargo pants and combat boots.

On his fifth lap in the hall, he did an about-face and stopped dead in his tracks, the air sucked from his lungs.

Leilani approached, wearing a white halter dress that hugged her figure down to just below her knees. The front plunged low, emphasizing the fullness of her breasts.

She'd left her hair hanging around her shoulders, pulled back on one side with a white flower above her ear.

"Wow," he said, incapable of forming a more fitting compliment for such beauty.

She gave him a tremulous smile. "Wow, yourself."

He grinned, remembered his manners and offered her his arm. "Sorry. You're so beautiful you took my breath and my words away."

"Nice recovery," she said, her dark cheeks flushing a soft red.

"Shall we?" He ushered her into the restaurant, where they were seated near a window overlooking the water. The sun was well on its way down, turning the scattered clouds incredible shades from pale pink to brilliant orange. But Angel had eyes only for the woman seated across from him.

She had him so tied in knots he forgot his excuse for getting her to join him for dinner.

Thankfully, the waiter was there to take their drink orders, giving him a moment to gather his scattered thoughts. By the time the waiter left, Angel had a tentative grip on his wits.

"I informed the guys they would be on duty tonight."

Leilani nodded. "I spoke with my boat captains. They'd like Reid and Dev to arrive at the Maalaea Harbor at ten o'clock. They'll meet them there and show them what needs to be done. Mainly, they need to be there to make sure no one else comes aboard. The crew will arrive at six in the morning to get the boat ready for the day's tours."

"I saw that your bus made it back from the shop," Angel said. He'd noticed it parked in front of the resort entrance with brand-new tires.

She smiled. "Thankfully, the shop delivered it, saving me a trip."

"What time will the waterfall tour leave tomorrow?" he asked.

"Ten," she said. "My guide, Olina, will be out front around nine-thirty with a roster of guests who've registered."

Angel pulled his cell phone from his pocket and held it up. "Do you mind?"

She shook her head. "Not at all. Please."

He quickly texted Reid and Dev, letting them

know the plan for the night shift. Then he texted Teller with the time he'd need to be out front for the ground tour. Once he sent the message, he placed his phone on vibrate and tucked it into his jacket for the remainder of the evening. He wanted to focus on the woman seated across from him.

"That leaves you," Angel said. "When will you head for the marina?"

"My captain will be by to pick me up around seven in the morning so that I can leave my car for Olina to take the children to school. Once the crew is on board, we don't actually need your team to hang around. You can let them get some rest."

"We're here to provide protection for you and your company. I'll send Reid back for rest and take over on the boat he's assigned. Dev expressed a desire to go out with the boat he'll be guarding. And I'd like to go with you to understand your business and responsibilities better. Someone from the outside looking in might see more than those closest to the problem."

Leilani cocked a dark eyebrow. "That's your pitch?"

He grinned. "Sounded good in my head." He dropped the smile and leaned closer. "You and your crew will be busy taking care of your guests. If someone is out to hurt your business, and maybe you, wouldn't it be better to have too many people looking out for you than not enough?"

"We've been operating short-staffed; thus, the need for me to fill in as a deckhand tomorrow." She sighed. "You're right. Having you and Dev on board tomorrow will help. I'll introduce you as deckhands. I don't want to scare the paying customers by telling them you're there to provide security."

"Good. Then I can drive you to the harbor tomorrow. Your captain won't have to swing by to pick you up."

"Are you sure? It would save him from backtracking to pick me up."

"Positive." He handed her his cell phone. "Let him know now so he can sleep in a little."

She called her boat captain and told him she had a ride to the harbor and that she'd meet him there in the morning. When she finished, she handed the cell phone to Angel. "Thank you."

The waiter arrived with their drinks and took their orders.

Leilani chose the grilled Mahi Mahi. Angel asked for the Mahi Mahi and the filet mignon.

The wine helped to ease Angel's nerves, making it easier to talk with Leilani about her life growing up on the island.

She seemed more comfortable talking about her family and the life she'd had before the fire.

"You said you owned an art gallery. Was art your major in college?" he asked.

"Yes," she answered.

"Were you more interested in representing other artists, or are you an artist yourself?"

She glanced out the window at the ocean as if the water held her memories. "Both." The word came out softly.

Angel sensed a deep sadness. "What mediums do you work in?"

She gazed away from the ocean and looked down at her hands. "Oil, watercolors, pen and ink, photography. Whatever captured the essence of the subject best. But mostly painting." She grimaced and looked across the table at him. "Enough about me. Tell me what it's like to be a Navy SEAL. That has to be much more exciting than life on an island."

Angel shook his head. "Have you painted since?"

She snorted softly. "Who has time? So many of my employees relied on their jobs. The art gallery and my studio are gone. The tours employ more people. I had to focus on getting those businesses up and running so that at least some of them could start earning a living again."

"Have you looked into renting a building in another town where you can open a gallery?" he asked. "One with room for a studio?"

She shook her head. "No. What's the point? I'm too busy working the tours to do anything else. We're still waiting for the authorities to open up Lahaina so that we can start rebuilding. They've started clearing the harbor. Hopefully, we'll be allowed in soon." She lifted her chin. "If you don't mind, I'd rather talk about something else."

Angel nodded. Hawk had warned him that the people affected by the fires might not want to be bombarded with questions. The media and tourists couldn't get enough and had pushed them past their usual friendly demeanor. "Fair enough." Taking his cue, Angel steered away from the Lahaina tragedy and talked about some of the places he'd been.

Their meals came, and they ate in silence for a while. When Leilani laid down her fork, she smiled. "That was some of the best Mahi Mahi I've had in a while. Did you know that the beef served here comes from the Big Island?"

"I have heard that the Big Island has one of the largest cattle ranches in the States. In fact, the Hawaiian branch of the Brotherhood Protectors is based on that ranch."

"Really?" Leilani's eyes widened. "How did Hank score that ranch for the Hawaii location?"

"He sent one of his guys out to provide protection for the ranch owner's daughter. The man he sent was a Navy SEAL but had prior experience in ranching. Apparently, the ranch owner's daughter wasn't keen on having a bodyguard, so Hawk, the guy Hank sent, hired on as a ranch hand. He saved the daughter's life. They fell in love, and the ranch owner offered to let him stay and start another branch of the Brotherhood there. It's been a few years in the making, but

Hank's finally staffing that branch. That's why we're here."

"Timing couldn't have been better for me," Leilani said.

"If they'd staffed it earlier, I might not have been assigned this location at this particular time," Angel said. "I might have gone to one of the others."

"Like Eagle Rock or West Yellowstone, Montana, or Fool's Gold, Colorado? Maybe even...what was the other?" Her brow furrowed and then cleared. "Bayou Mambaloa. That one sounded interesting."

He grinned. "You did your homework."

She nodded. "I'm impressed with how many different offices have been established." Her lips twisted. "At the same time, it's sad that there's such a need for protection. Why can't people get along? We shouldn't have to be afraid that someone will attack us."

"True," Angel said. "But I've been in worse places."

Leilani nodded. "I can imagine."

"I'm just glad Hank let my team come as a package. If we'd gone to one of the other locations, we might have been split up. It's nice that we'll stay together. At least we'll work out of the same office. Our jobs could take us anywhere." He laid down his fork and napkin. Though the meal was complete, he didn't want the time with Leilani to end. "It's a beautiful night. Would you like to have a drink out by the pool? They're supposed to have live music and dancing." He nodded toward her. "It would be a shame to put that dress to bed early."

She laughed, her hand smoothing over the material. "If you only knew what I had to do to find a dress on such short notice."

"Tell me," he urged.

Her lips curled in a secretive smile. "And take away the mystery? No way." She lifted her chin. "But you're right. This dress deserves a little more nightlife."

Angel grinned, rose and helped Leilani to her feet. With a hand at the small of her back, he led her through the restaurant and outside where a small band played on the patio near the infinity pool.

He ordered drinks at the bar and found chairs at the farthest end of the patio with an ocean vista and an endless view of the stars.

He sat for a while, absorbing the music and enjoying being with Leilani more than he had thought possible on such a short acquaintance. Being with her felt natural, unpretentious and really good.

"I don't think I've been this relaxed in a long time," she whispered.

"Same," Angel said.

She took another sip and raised her face to the sky. "Must be the wine."

"For me, it's the company," he said, risking scaring her off. But it was true.

She raised her empty hand toward him.

He took it, curling his fingers around hers, holding her lightly. If she wanted to pull away, she could. This woman had enough on her plate. She didn't need to feel trapped.

"Thank you for inviting me to dinner," she said. "It was nice to share a meal with someone."

"Don't you have friends?" he asked.

"I do. Olina, my friend and one of my employees, lives in the suite beside mine. I eat with her and her three children when I can. But I'm usually too late. They eat earlier so she can get the kids to bed at a reasonable hour. They have school." Leilani smiled. "I imagine she's tucking them in now. They've been little troopers, considering what they've been through. Palili still has nightmares about drowning."

"Were they some of the people who escaped into the ocean?" he asked.

Leilani nodded. "By the time Olina and I got to them, it was the only way out of the fire."

Angel's chest tightened. He'd just learned another amazing thing about this woman. Not only had she lost her home and belongings, she'd almost lost her life. Instead of looking out for herself, she'd helped save the lives of a woman and her three children. Leilani was what heroes were made of. He squeezed her hand gently. "I'm sorry they had to go through what they did. It can't be easy getting over it."

The band eased into a slow, romantic song.

"I like that song," Leilani murmured.

Angel pushed to his feet, still holding onto her hand. "Would you like to dance?"

Her brow furrowed.

He cocked an eyebrow. "You know that dress deserves at least one dance to get your money's worth."

Leilani laughed and let him help her to her feet. "By all means, I need to get my money's worth out of this dress."

He pulled her into his arms and moved slowly to the rhythm of the music.

She rested one hand in his and the other on his arm; her eyes closed and a smile played at the corners of her lips.

While she danced with her eyes closed, Angel studied her beautiful face. Hers was an exotic beauty, a product of her Pacific Islander heritage. Dark skin, dark eyes and dark shiny hair spilling down her back, brushing against his hand. More than anything, Angel wanted to kiss those full, sensual lips.

Her petite body felt fragile next to his large frame. But he knew her small size contained a fierce spirit, undaunted by tragedy. Though he'd only known her a few hours, he could already tell a few days with her would not be enough.

All too soon, the song ended.

Leilani's eyes blinked open. "That was nice. The whole evening was nice. But I should call it a night. We have a busy day tomorrow. And after the snorkeling tour, I have to do some errands for my cousin's wedding."

He hooked her arm through the crook of her elbow. "Thank you for having dinner with me. I'll walk you back to your room."

"You don't have to," she said.

"I know. But I want to." He stared down at her. "That is, if you're okay with it."

She smiled. "I'd like that."

Together, they walked through the resort and down the path to the section where Leilani lived.

When they arrived at her door, she slipped her hand out of the crook of his arm. "Thanks again for dinner and dancing."

She looked up at him, her face bathed in moonlight, her lips turned up in a smile.

"I want to kiss you," he whispered.

Her eyes flared, and her hand rose to rest on his chest. "What's stopping you?"

"Not a damned thing." His pulse quickened as his arms came up around her. He lowered his head.

She rose on her toes.

His lips were a breath away from hers.

"Leilani?" a female voice called out from the door next to hers.

Angel raised his head.

Leilani stepped out of his arms.

The moment was lost.

"Olina?" Leilani frowned. "Is everything all right?"

The woman shook her head. "It's Palili. She had another one of her nightmares, and she's asking for you." Olina looked from Leilani to Angel. "I can tell her you're not home."

"No," Leilani said. "Don't do that. We'll come." She took Angel's hand. "Olina, this is Angel. Angel, meet Olina."

Olina frowned. "Are you sure? I don't want to ruin your evening."

Angel wasn't about to confirm that Olina had already ruined the finale to a wonderful date with her beautiful friend. "Not at all. We'd love to help." And he really did want to help the little girl despite having missed a kiss he'd been wishing for since Leilani had appeared in that dress.

Olina led the way into one of the bedrooms in the two-bedroom suite. The room had two double beds. A little boy slept in one of the beds, undisturbed by the sobbing little girl curled up next to the oldest daughter.

Leilani went to the little girl and laid a hand on her shoulder. "Palili, sweetheart, it's me, Lani."

The little girl rolled over and opened red-rimmed eyes. "Lani?"

As soon as Leilani sat on the edge of the bed, the girl threw herself into her arms and cried some more.

"It's okay, baby," she said, stroking the child's hair and her back.

"I c-couldn't s-swim," she said. "And the water was so c-cold."

"It was just a dream, sweetie," Leilani said. "You're awake now. Warm and dry. In your bed with Mamo, your mama and Noa. And look," Leilani placed a finger beneath Palili's chin and raised her head. "Check out my handsome date."

Palili blinked back tears and stared up at Angel. "He's so tall," she whispered and buried her face against Leilani's chest. "Doesn't that scare you?"

Leilani laughed softly. "No, he makes me feel safe, knowing I'm with him. Say hello to him. He doesn't bite. I promise."

Palili ventured a glance at him.

Angel held out his hand. "Palili, my name is Angelo. It's nice to meet you."

Palili looked to Leilani.

Leilani nodded.

The little girl took Angel's hand. "Nice to meet you."

Angel gave her little hand a shake and let go. With a smile down at the pair, he waved toward Leilani. "Did Leilani show you the dress she wore for our date?"

Palili shook her head.

"Stand up, Leilani," Olina urged.

"Yes, please," the older girl said. "We want to see the dress."

Leilani looked down into Palili's eyes. "Is that okay?"

Palili nodded. "I want to see the dress, too."

Leilani untangled herself from Palili's arms and stood, smoothing a hand over her dress. "What do you think?"

Palili's eyes widened. "You're beautiful."

"You are," the older daughter agreed.

"Where on earth did you find it?" Olina asked.

Leilani pressed a finger to her lips. "It's a secret." She leaned close to Palili. "I'll tell you tomorrow." When she straightened, she held out a hand to the little girl. "Feeling better?"

Palili nodded, taking Leilani's hand.

Leilani squeezed her fingers. "Sometimes, you have to wake all the way to chase away the bad dreams. I know. I have nightmares, too."

Palili's eyes widened. "You do?"

"I do," Leilani said.

"So do I," Angel admitted.

"What do you do to make them go away?" Palili directed her question toward Angel.

"I turn on a light and sit up. I feel better as soon as I'm awake. Sometimes, I know it's a nightmare, even as it's happening. I make myself wake up to chase it away."

"I know it's a nightmare," Palili said, "but it feels so real. Like it's happening all over again."

"Next time, try to wake yourself up," Leilani said.

Angel nodded. "Sit up in bed. Turn on the light."

"That's right." Leilani nodded toward the other two children. "You'll see your sister and brother and know it was just a bad dream."

Palili yawned and lay back against the pillow. "I'll try." She looked up at Angel. "I like you, Mr. Angelo. Are you going to marry Lani?"

"Palili." Her mother shook her head. "They just met today."

Palili shrugged. "Lani's wearing a white dress. Mr. Angelo is wearing a suit. They look like they're going to get married." She yawned. "Could you wait until morning? I'm tired."

Lani laughed and bent to hug the little girl. "I'll wait. Get some sleep, baby. You're safe."

Palili closed her eyes. "You're right, Lani. He makes me feel safe, too."

The older sister stared up at Angel. "He makes me feel safe, too. You should keep him."

Lani reached out and brushed the hair off the older daughter's forehead. "Go to sleep, Mamo," she said. "Know that I love you."

Leilani stood for a few moments longer, staring down at the girls. When they both settled into the deep breathing of sleep, Leilani crossed to the other bed where the little boy slept soundly and pressed a kiss to his forehead.

The three adults backed out of the room. Olina pulled the door halfway closed and walked with

Leilani and Angel to the door of the suite. "Thanks," she said. "You always make her feel better. I'm sorry we interrupted your date."

"Don't be sorry." Leilani touched the woman's arm. "I hate that she's still having nightmares."

"Me, too," Olina said. "It takes time to recover."

"In so many ways." Leilani hugged the woman. "Don't hesitate to call me if you need anything."

Olina closed the door, leaving Leilani and Angel to walk back to Leilani's door.

"Thank you for everything. You really do make a girl feel safe. No matter how young or old." She leaned up on her toes and brushed her lips across his.

Before he could deepen the kiss, she turned away, flashed her key card over the door lock and disappeared into her suite, closing the door between them.

Damn, he'd missed his second chance at a real kiss.

He had to think kissing Leilani wasn't meant to be. Not that night, anyway. Maybe that wasn't such a bad thing. The near-miss kiss could be an even greater temptation, making the next time all the more exciting.

He'd go with that thought and look forward to his next date with the petite Hawaiian beauty.

In the meantime, a cold shower would have to do. It was that, or he would be awake all night or have entirely different kinds of dreams than the nightmares plaguing Palili.

Angel headed for his room, his step lighter. He slowed as an image of the slashed tires flashed through his mind. The night with Leilani had been pretty awesome, but it didn't erase the fact that someone was trying to put her out of business.

He didn't like the fact that someone had already struck twice. Although diesel in an engine was destructive, slashing tires had involved a knife or something equally sharp. A more violent attack in Angel's mind. Could the next attack target the business owner herself?

He pictured Leilani in her sexy white dress and frowned at the idea of someone plunging a knife into her. As quickly as the image surfaced, he pushed it away. He wouldn't let that happen. The more he got to know Leilani, the more he liked her.

Protecting Leilani could turn out to be a different kind of challenge altogether. His gut told him that not only was her business in danger, but she might be as well. He'd learned through experience to listen to his gut.

Someone would need to be with her twenty-four-seven to keep her safe.

That someone needed to be him.

When he arrived at his building, a shadow detached itself from the wall beside his door.

Angel dropped into a defensive stance, adrenaline racing through his system.

"Relax," a voice said. "It's me, Teller." His team-mate stepped into the starlight.

Angel straightened, drew in a deep breath and let it out slowly. "Dude, I could've killed you."

"I doubt it. If I were out to take you down, you'd be dead already. What happened to situational awareness?"

Angel shook his head. "I was thinking."

"That'll get you killed."

"Tell me about it." Angel waved his key card over the lock. "Can I offer you a beer?"

"No thanks. I came to deliver a message from Hawk."

"Oh yeah?" Angel led the way into his room. "What message?"

"He tried to call you. When he couldn't get you on the phone, he called the rest of us. Since the others are guarding boats tonight, I was tagged with getting with you to do a video call with our new boss."

"Sounds serious. I'll bring him up on my laptop." Angel strode to his computer, turned it on and pulled up two chairs. He sank into one. Teller settled in the other.

He placed the video call and waited for Hawk to answer.

Hawk responded on the first ring. "Cortez, Osgood. Couldn't you guys stand any more than a couple of days of R&R without looking for work?"

Angel nodded. "Let's just say it landed in our laps."

"Correction," Teller said. "She landed in Cortez's lap."

Hawk grinned. "It happens. I touched base with Hank a couple of hours ago. He and I are in agreement. You're to stay on this job until it's solved. If that means you're on Maui for more than a week, so be it. Hank and I are still lining up work for all of you. I can get the others started while you're wrapping up Ms. Kealoha's case."

"So, it's official? Ms. Kealoha is our first client with the Brotherhood Protectors?" Teller asked.

"That's right. Let me know if you need anything in the way of weapons, communications equipment or tracking devices. I can get those sent over by airplane."

"Hopefully, we won't need all that," Angel said, "but it's good to know it's available."

"You also have access to Hank's computer guy, Swede. He's a master at data mining. You can have him look up information about people, corporations, bank accounts and government records. He has ways of getting the information you need to know."

"Have him do some digging on Makai Kealoha."

"Any relation to the client?" Hawk asked.

"He's her cousin," Teller responded.

"Could be some jealousy over inheritance involved," Angel explained. "Also, look for a broker named Peter Brentwood. Find out who he represents. He's been badgering Ms. Kealoha to sell her property in Lahaina. Then have Swede look up Buddy Akina, a Maui resident who's been actively campaigning against the return of tourism to the island."

"I'll pass these names on to Swede," Hawk said. "Again, if you need anything, I can get people or equipment to you ASAP."

"Thanks," Angel said. "Each of us has a handgun should we need a firearm. If we need more, I'll take you up on delivering some things. For now, we're all right."

"Okay, then," Hawk nodded. "Welcome to the Brotherhood Protectors."

CHAPTER 6

LEILANI HAD STOOD with her back against the door long after she'd closed it, straining to hear the sound of his knock, hoping he'd come after her to claim the kiss he'd lost to a child's nightmare. When he didn't knock, she kicked herself for running away instead of initiating a kiss he could return.

She'd gone to bed frustrated at first. But after reminding herself of how wonderful it had been to share a meal with the man and then dance in his arms under the stars, she closed her eyes with a smile.

Not long after she fell asleep, she dreamed of lifting a paintbrush and touching it to the canvas she'd been painting for the governor's mansion. It was so close to being finished she didn't want to stop until it was done.

A clock ticked loudly on the wall, and shouts sounded

in the street, drawing her to the window. When she looked out, the bright blue Maui sky was gone. In its place were black, billowing clouds of smoke.

Olina called out from downstairs in the gallery, "Lani, we have to go."

"I can't leave until I finish the painting," Leilani said.

"We have to save the children," Olina shouted. "Help me."

"But—" Leilani stared at the most beautiful painting she'd ever created. Deep in her heart, she knew she'd never paint anything quite as perfect again. How could she leave it?

"Please," Olina begged. "My babies need you."

Leilani picked up the painting and threw it out the window. It burst into flames before it hit the ground and was carried off in the wind, one giant, burning ember, landing on the roof of the next building. The one that Windsong Tours operated out of. Immediately, the entire roof exploded in flames.

Leilani ran down the stairs and out into the street. Olina was there with her three children. Mamo held Noa; Palili held her mother's hand. They followed others trudging along Front Street.

"Where are you going?" Leilani yelled.

"We have to get out of town," a police officer said as he walked by. "Must evacuate."

"But you're heading into the firestorm," Leilani said. "Stop them."

"Must evacuate," the officer said, his face already gray with ash.

"No!" Leilani cried. "Don't go that way. Head for the water."

Olina and the kids didn't listen or couldn't hear her screaming. They kept walking like zombies, vacant-eyed, disappearing into the black cloud of smoke.

Leilani ran after them, scooped Palili up in her arms, took Mamo's hand and dragged her toward the harbor. "Olina! Get to the water!" she cried over her shoulder.

Leilani dragged the children toward the harbor, her feet moving as if anchored in quicksand. When she finally reached the water, she pushed the kids in and told Palili to hold onto her sister's hand. "I'm going back for your mother."

Leilani raced into the smoke, eyes and lungs burning. She couldn't see any more than a foot in front of her. Holding her arms out, she felt her way, praying she was heading in the right direction. When she finally bumped into someone, she sobbed with relief. It was Olina.

"I can't find my kids," Olina said, tears streaming down her face. "I can't save them."

"They're in the water," Leilani said. "Come with me. I'll take you to them."

Leilani led Olina to the harbor, the heat bearing down on them.

When they reached the water, Leilani couldn't see the children. The tide churned, tossing waves of ash against the shore.

A scream sounded in the distance. Through the haze of smoke, Leilani caught a glimpse of Mamo holding Noa, and Palili drifting away from them, arms flailing, her little head dipping below the surface.

"Palili!" Leilani yelled. "I'm coming!" She dove into the water and swam with all her heart. No matter how hard she swam, she didn't seem to be getting nearer. Palili's head dipped beneath the surface one last time and didn't come back up.

"No!" Leilani cried. This couldn't be happening. It had to be a nightmare. A dream that she could wake from. None of this was happening.

Leilani stopped swimming and tread water as she concentrated.

"Wake up," she said aloud.

Ash-laden waves splashed over her, pushing her under.

"Wake up!"

Leilani sat up in bed, her body drenched in sweat, her pulse pounding. Darkness surrounded her like black smoke. She didn't want to breathe and inhale it into her lungs.

Desperate for air, she leaned over and switched on the lamp on the nightstand. As soon as the light chased away the darkness, Leilani sucked air into her starving lungs. She filled them with air and then released it all in a rush.

"Just a dream," she whispered and hugged her pillow to her chest, rocking back and forth in an attempt to calm her racing heart. "It was just a dream."

For the next fifteen minutes, she sat upright in her bed until sleep dragged at her eyelids. She was afraid to go to sleep and end up back in the ashy sea where Palili had sunk beneath the surface. If she stayed awake, Palili would live, safe in her bed next door. If she slept, Palili would be lost forever.

So, she rocked until she dropped off out of sheer exhaustion and slept like the dead until the incessant ringing of her alarm jerked her awake.

Leilani dragged herself out of bed and into her bathroom, where she splashed water on her face until she'd washed the remaining fog of sleep from her eyes.

She made a note to herself to give Palili extra hugs the next time she saw her. Just to prove to herself she hadn't drowned like she had in her nightmare.

When she glanced again at the clock, she freaked. With less than five minutes to dress and brush her hair and teeth, she sprang into action, fighting off the lingering weight of her nightmare.

Leilani had just shoved her feet into her tennis shoes when a knock sounded on her door. She ran to answer it, fully prepared to throw herself into Angel's waiting arms.

When she flung open the door, it wasn't Angel standing there.

She blinked in confusion at Peter Brentwood and

half a dozen other men crowding in on her. "What the hell's going on?"

"I got word you were ready to sell." Peters waved a sheath of documents in her face. "I brought the contract. All you have to do is sign, and it's done."

"That's bullshit," another man Leilani had seen before stepped around Peter with his own set of documents. "I got the message to bring a contract this morning that Ms. Kealoha was ready to accept our offer."

"I don't know what kind of game you all are playing?" another man said. "Ms. Kealoha agreed to sell to my client. I got a message from her last night, asking me to bring the contract at seven this morning."

The men all started talking at once, their voices rising.

Leilani pinched the bridge of her nose, a dull ache growing at the base of her skull. "Enough," she said.

When the men didn't stop talking over each other, she drew in a deep breath, ready to scream.

Before she let loose, a tall man with broad shoulders, wearing a baseball cap pulled low over his forehead, muscled his way through the crowd of brokers.

"Hey!" one man protested.

Another lurched to the side. "Watch it, man!"

A third man spun when a shoulder rammed into him. "What the hell?"

When the bulldozer of a man reached Leilani, he slipped his arm around her waist. Using his body as a shield and a battering ram, he shoved his way back through the arguing brokers.

He kept walking until they reached the parking lot and dark SUV.

When he finally stopped, Leilani flung her arms around Angel's waist and buried her face against his chest. "Thank you," she said, her voice muffled by his polo shirt.

"What was with the circus so early in the morning?" he asked as he held the passenger door open for Leilani to climb in.

She waited for him to get into the driver's seat before leaning her head back against the seat. "I don't know what happened. Apparently, they all got a message, supposedly from me, saying that I was ready to sign contracts to sell my property."

"I take it you sent no such message," Angel said as he started the engine.

Leilani shook her head. "Not unless I did it in my sleep. But after last night's nightmare, I'd believe anything."

Angel glanced over at her. "Bad one?"

She closed her eyes. "The worst one so far."

As Angel drove out of the parking lot, he held out his hand.

Leilani took the hand, glad for something to hold onto. She could have used a hand to hold when she'd been drowning in her nightmare. Holding his now helped more than she could have imagined.

"Do you want to talk about it?" he asked.

"No," she said. "It's enough that you came to my rescue. Someone really has it in for me. Not only does he want my businesses to fail, he wants me to sell my only connection to my hometown."

"I spoke with my boss, Hawk, after I left you last night and told him to have Hank's computer guy look into Peter Brentwood and Buddy Akina." He shrugged. "I don't know that it will lead to anything, but it's a start."

Leilani shook her head. "It doesn't make sense. If the broker is sabotaging my business to break me financially and force me to sell rather than claim bankruptcy, why would he send messages to all the other agents that I was ready to sell?"

"No, it doesn't make sense." Angel frowned as he navigated the road ahead. "What about Buddy Akina? What does he have to gain by destroying your business and forcing you to sell? Wouldn't that defeat his purpose to keep big corporations from buying up Lahaina and building the next Honolulu on Maui?"

"Unless he wants me to get angry at the people who want to buy the land to develop it, and I decide to go the other route and donate it to the state?" She shook her head. "That would be too much of a stretch."

"What about your cousin?" Angel asked. "Would he gain anything by forcing you out?"

"Absolutely nothing."

"He's your only living relative. Would he inherit the land if you were to die?"

"No. I have it in my will that if I die, the land will be donated to the state to build a park that helps preserve the beauty and culture of Maui and our ancestors." She turned to Angel. "Makai would inherit nothing."

Angel frowned. "Does he know that?"

"No," Leilani said. "No one knows but me and the attorney I hired to draft my will. And he's not on Maui. I went to Oahu to get it done." She sighed. "I really don't think Makai is behind what's going on. We were really close growing up. He wouldn't hurt me."

"Greed makes people do terrible things," Angel said.

"Not Makai," she said.

When they arrived at Maalaea Harbor, Leilani showed Angel the small building they'd rented while they operated their boat tours out of the harbor.

"Besides snorkeling tours, we do the occasional dive trips and contract exclusive trips to people who want to hire the boat for a day of diving and spearfishing. We haven't offered diving excursions yet because our certified divers lost their homes in the fire and moved in with family on Oahu and the Big Island. I'm certified, but it's been a while since I've led a dive trip. For now, we're starting out slow with snorkeling."

She led him to the two boats Windsong Tours had moored at the harbor, Windsong I and Windsong II. "Windsong III was our catamaran. My captains could only get two of the crafts out of Lahaina Harbor in time to escape the fire. The catamaran didn't make it."

The crews were hard at work, preparing the boats for the day's trips.

Dev waved from the deck of Windsong II as he helped lay out the life vests in a neat row, ready for the guests when they came aboard at eight o'clock. He seemed to be fitting in with the other deckhand, who was filling the barrel they used to soak the masks and snorkels to disinfect them before each use.

When Leilani boarded, Angel followed.

The captain and Dev joined her on deck.

"How did it go last night?" she asked Dev.

He shook his head. "I slept on the deck with one eye open. Nothing moved. No one approached the boat. It was a quiet night full of nothing but stars."

"That's good," Leilani turned to the blond-haired, blue-eyed captain of Windsong II. "Captain Dave, this is Angelo Cortez. He's a new deckhand who'll be working with me on the Windsong I. Angel, Captain Dave Smith."

The two men shook hands.

"Prior service?" Angel asked as he released the captain's hand.

Captain Dave nodded. "Eight years in the Navy,

and I never left the land." He snorted. "I had to leave the Navy to get back to the water." He cocked an eyebrow. "You?"

"Also, Navy," Angel said. "Spent more time in the desert than in the water."

"Glad to have you as part of the Windsong crew. You'll like working with Captain Ako. He's a good man."

"Thank you." Angel nodded to Dev without saying anything.

Dev nodded back.

Leilani left the boat and boarded Windsong I.

Captain Ako and the only other deckhand on board met her on the deck.

Captain Ako shook Leilani's hand. "Glad to have you aboard for today's tour."

"Glad to be here," Leilani said. "How's Suzy?"

His lips twisted. "Butting heads with her mother and counting the days until she and the kids can come home."

Leilani smiled. "Amos and Kalea getting along in school on the Big Island?"

"As best they can. Amos drove his kindergarten teacher up the wall for the first couple of weeks until he finally settled down. Kalea's already established herself as the teacher's pet in her third-grade class." He sighed. "They're a lot of work, but I miss them like crazy. It's too quiet without them."

"Give Suzy my love next time you talk." She

touched his arm. "I wish I could tell you it'll get better soon."

"But you can't." He nodded. "We just have to take it one day at a time."

Leilani stepped back. "Captain Ako, this is our new deckhand for the day, Angelo Cortez. He'll be working with me to learn the ropes. He's friends with Reid and Dev."

Captain Ako held out his hand. "Welcome aboard."

"Thank you, Captain," Angel said.

Leilani smiled at the only other deckhand. "Josh, Angelo. Angelo, Josh."

Angel shook hands with Josh. "Nice to meet you."

Leilani got to work, showing Angel what needed to be done to prepare for the guests who would arrive within the hour.

He worked quickly and efficiently, even taking the initiative to clean places that needed attention without having them pointed out.

Leilani stowed the catered continental breakfast and the trays of food that would be served as a buffet for lunch. Beer and soda were loaded into ice chests. She checked the bottles of alcohol arranged behind the bar and made note of the ones that would need to be replaced before the next day's tours.

By the time the resort shuttle dropped off the guests, the boat was ready.

Leilani stood on the dock, clipboard in hand,

checking the names against the reservations, one at a time. She smiled and chatted with each person, making them feel more comfortable. The mood was festive, and the people were excited to get out on the water and experience some of the sea life Maui had to offer.

Once everyone was on board, Josh and Angel handed each person a life vest. Josh demonstrated how to wear the vest.

Captain Ako set the boat in motion, easing away from the dock and through the harbor.

With the sun shining down, Leilani drew in a breath of warm, clean air. If a person didn't know the recent history, he would never guess that this idyllic place had suffered such a horrendous tragedy that had killed a hundred people and forever changed the lives of so many more.

Heading south, the captain took the boat to Molokini Crater, the ancient volcano with only a crescent-shaped rim protruding dramatically from the water.

In the hour it took to get there, Leilani served drinks, croissants and fruit cups, while the guys fitted guests with masks, snorkels and fins.

The captain positioned the Windsong I in the protected cover formed by the crescent of the volcano, lining up with eight other tour boats, spaced out to give their guests room to swim alongside their boats.

Leilani gave a short safety briefing, informing the guests that they couldn't touch the wildlife or the reefs. "See with your eyes, not your hands," she said with a smile. "Help us protect our reefs and its inhabitants. We have over two hundred fifty local species of sea life. You should see black durgon triggerfish, locally known as the *humuhumu 'ele 'ele*. Then there's the largest and most colorful reef fish, the parrotfish or *Uhu*. Plus, there's Hawaii's state fish, the Lagoon Trigger Fish, lovingly called the *Humuhumunukunukuapua`a*." She cocked an eyebrow and looked around at the people seated on benches, fins already fitted on bare feet and holding their snorkels. "Anyone want to give that name a try?"

People laughed.

Her gaze swept toward Angel. She caught him grinning. His smile made her day even brighter.

"Josh will be in the water with you if you need help with anything and to point out interesting things you might not notice. You'll have an hour here. Enjoy."

People waddled to the back of the boat and entered the water one at a time. Josh joined them, leading a bright orange life preserver donut by a rope.

The captain stayed on the upper deck at the helm, leaving Leilani and Angel alone on the lower deck.

Suddenly shy, she busied herself rearranging items behind the bar.

Angel stared out at the boats around them. He waved at Dev on Windsong II as Captain Dave maneuvered into a position beside their boat.

With his back to Leilani, she had the opportunity to study the man. He wore a plain white T-shirt that stretched snuggly over broad shoulders. His swim trunks had a nautical theme in varying shades of blue. With his short, sandy blond hair and amazing tan, he could have been a swimwear model. He had everything it took to make a woman look twice and maybe drool a little.

At that moment, he turned, his light blue eyes twinkling in the sunshine as he caught her staring at him. A smile tugged at the corners of his lips. "Can I help?"

"No," she said quickly and ducked to check the drinks that didn't need to be checked in the cooler, her cheeks burning. All she could think about was the brush of a kiss she'd given him the night before. Had he been intrigued? Teased? Disappointed?

God, she wished she'd stuck around to show him what kind of kiss she was really capable of.

When she finally raised her head, she muffled a squeal.

Angel stood on the other side of the bar, less than a foot away. He reached across the counter and took her hand in his. "Thanks again for having dinner with me last night. It was the highlight of my stay on

Maui. So far." He raised her hand to his lips and pressed his lips to the backs of her knuckles.

Her knees melted as a rush of heat coiled at her center. "I enjoyed it. I hope I didn't bore you."

He chuckled. "Far from it. I love getting to know you." His gaze went to where his hand still held hers. "I have only one regret."

Her brow puckered. "You do?"

He nodded, his head coming up, his eyes staring into hers. "That I didn't get to kiss you back."

CHAPTER 7

TIME STOOD STILL for a moment as Leilani fell into the smoky depths of Angel's blue gaze. She turned her hand over and curled her fingers around his.

"You see," Angel said, "my date kissed me and ran."

"Silly woman," Leilani whispered, her breath lodged in her lungs.

His brow twisted. "I wondered if she was afraid of me."

She turned her head from side to side. "Maybe she was afraid of herself."

"Why?" he asked softly.

"Confused. Barely knows him. They only have a short time together. Afraid he might not be as attracted to her as she is to him." She snorted. "Out of practice."

His eyes flared. "Oh, he's attracted. She's beautiful, brave, intelligent and kind."

"He's leaving after a week."

"All the more reason to kiss sooner than later." He tugged her hand, pulling her toward him as he leaned over the bar.

"Hey, Leilani," Josh called out from the water. "Trade this mask for another, will you?" He tossed a mask onto the deck. "It leaks."

Angel shook his head and let go of Leilani's hand. "At this rate, I'm beginning to think we can't catch a break. I'll get this." He turned, grabbed another mask from the barrel and handed it over the side to Josh.

"You should come in," Josh said. "I've never seen as many fish in one trip as today."

Leilani came to stand beside Angel. "You should go."

He frowned. "I'm not here to play in the water."

She waved her hand around at the boats parked in a line. "Nothing's going to happen in a bay full of witnesses. Go. See why people love to come to Maui and why we're so proud of our islands. I'll be fine."

He held out his hand. "I won't go unless you come with me."

Her eyes narrowed. Normally, she stayed on board, getting things ready for lunch. But she was caught up. If she stayed on board, she'd just be standing around wishing she'd gone with Angel.

Leilani smiled. "Why not?" With a quick movement, she yanked her Windsong polo shirt over her head and stepped out of her shoes and shorts, glad she'd decided to wear her bikini under her work clothes at the last minute.

Angel shucked his T-shirt, exposing an impressive, muscular chest that made Leilani forget for a moment how to breathe.

Wow.

What she wouldn't give to run her fingers over his skin and test how solid those muscles were.

She grabbed a mask and snorkel, tossed them to Angel and selected one for herself. The sooner they got into the chilly water of the Pacific, the sooner her libido would cool, and she could think straight again.

Angel snagged a couple of pairs of fins, handing her one set. They sat side by side on the bench and slid their feet into the fins.

When she stood, she yelled, "Captain Ako, I'm going in with the others. You're alone on board."

Captain Ako came to the edge of the upper deck and gave her a mock salute. "Yes, ma'am. Have fun."

She fit her mask over her face and duck-walked to the back of the boat. "Last one in is a rotten—"

Before she got the last word out, a flash of man-flesh flew by her as Angel performed an awesome belly-flop into the sea.

Leilani laughed, held onto her mask and stepped over the side, dropping down into the water.

After standing in the warm air and sunshine, the chill of the Pacific Ocean took her breath away.

Leilani surfaced and looked around for Angel but didn't find him.

A hand grabbed her ankle and yanked her downward. She barely had a chance to catch a breath before she submerged.

Angel's hands climbed up her body and wrapped around her, his fingers firm against her naked skin. Then they surfaced to breathe.

As much as she wanted to get close to his incredible body, a mask and snorkel were far from sexy and not at all conducive to any kind of foreplay. She made a note to herself to take Angel swimming at the resort's beach. No snorkel or mask.

Suits optional.

Maybe that night. A shiver rippled through her that had nothing to do with the chill temperature of the water.

With only a little time left before she had to get out, dry off and be ready to serve the guests, Leilani swam beside Angel, pointing out the different varieties of fish she'd talked about earlier, also sighting a pufferfish, a school of yellow tang, a spotted trunkfish and the long, thin trumpetfish.

Aware of the passage of time, Leilani stayed close to the boat, wanting to be on deck when the first passengers came back aboard.

When Leilani surfaced, Angel came up beside her.

She removed the snorkel from her mouth. "I need to get back to work. You can stay longer if you like."

He shook his head. "I'm with you."

They swam back to the boat, removed their fins and tossed them onto deck before they climbed out of the water.

Angel took her gear and stowed it where it belonged.

Leilani stepped behind the bar, where they kept extra towels for the crew to use to dry off. She grabbed two and threw one to Angel.

Within moments, she'd dried her skin and absorbed as much water as she could from her hair and bikini. She had just pulled on her polo shirt and shorts and taken her position behind the bar when the first passenger climbed out of the water.

Josh rounded up the rest of the folks, herding them toward the boat and then assisting them with fin removal prior to their climbing the ladder up into the boat.

Leilani handed out drinks to those who wanted them.

When the last passenger was aboard, Josh secured the boat, and the captain sailed out of Molokini Crater, moving on to their next stop, the Coral Gardens.

The guests talked excitedly about the different fish they'd seen while snorkeling. One couple had seen an octopus. Everyone was happy and ready to do it again.

The Windsong II followed a few minutes behind them, a small spec in the distance.

Leilani couldn't stop smiling. Not only was the tour going well, but every time she looked at Angel, he was looking back at her. He'd admitted he'd wanted to kiss her the night before and had almost kissed her leaning over the bar today. It was going to happen. Of that, she was convinced.

And she couldn't wait.

Snorkeling in the Coral Gardens was a hit when three green sea turtles showed up, hanging around for a good twenty minutes before they swam off.

By then, the guests were hungry and ready for lunch. Leilani had arranged trays of deli sandwiches, pasta salad, assorted bags of chips and cookies across the counter.

Guests worked their way through the line, buffet-style, while Leilani, Josh and Angel got them the drinks they wanted.

Most of the adults opted for beer and mixed drinks. The few kids on board drank sodas. Josh turned on the music, playing songs from the '70s to the present.

By the time lunch was over, the guests were in full party mode, singing along to the lyrics and consuming more alcohol.

Leilani, Josh and Angel gathered the trash and stowed the leftover food while the captain maneuvered the boat out of the bay, heading back to Maalaea Harbor.

Leilani stayed busy keeping up with drink orders. When she glanced up long enough to locate Angel, she found him staring out to sea, his brow furrowed, his body tense.

She looked past him to what appeared to be a long, thin jet boat, the kind people called cigar boats. It was moving fast, skimming across the water as if flying through the air.

Leilani frowned.

It was headed straight for the Windsong I at full speed.

Angel moved quickly toward Josh. "See that boat?"

Josh turned. "What boat?" At that moment, he must have seen the oncoming cigar boat. "Holy shit." He spun and raced up the ladder to the top deck, where the captain steered the boat full of people.

Angel stared for a moment longer, then spun toward Leilani. Should they trust the speed boat driver to turn? Or brace for impact?

Leilani shook her head and rushed toward the passengers on the side of the boat closest to the speeding cigar boat. "Folks, listen up! I need you to move off the benches and get on the floor of the boat."

The people looked at her, confused by her

request. They had their backs to the oncoming threat.

"Why?" a man asked.

A woman pulled her child close. "What's going on?"

Leilani didn't have time to explain.

Angel stepped forward. "Just do it!" he yelled, his voice booming over the engine's roar. "Now!"

"And secure the buckles on your life vests," Leilani added.

Their eyes wide, everyone tumbled to the deck, crowded together, a tangle of arms and legs.

Out of the corner of his eye, Angel saw the cigar boat turn at the last minute, skimming sideways across the water, still headed toward them.

He grabbed Leilani around the waist and sank to the deck, using his body to shield hers.

The cigar boat rammed into the side of the Windsong I, tossing the bigger boat like a buoy bobbing in a raging storm.

Passengers screamed, sliding across the deck and crashing into the people trapped against the benches.

When the boat rocked back the other way, they slid in the opposite direction, clinging to each other.

Angel held Leilani tightly around the middle, his legs wrapped around her hips and legs. As they slid across the deck, they didn't have the benches in front of them to slow them down.

Angel extended his legs. When his feet hit the side

of the boat, he bent his knees, absorbing the impact. If he hadn't been holding onto Leilani, she might have been catapulted headfirst into the wall.

No sooner had they slid into the starboard side then the boat rocked violently in the opposite direction, flinging the passengers back across the deck.

Angel's back hit the port wall, his body cushioning Leilani's.

More screams cleaved the air.

The boat continued to rock, less and less violently, until it came to a stop.

Leilani started to get up.

Angel held onto her. "Stay down until the captain gives us the all-clear," he said, his voice carrying over the frightened sobs of the women and children.

Those who had been trying to rise ducked down again.

Moments later, Captain Ako's voice boomed from the upper deck. "It's gone." He looked over the edge of the upper deck. "Everybody all right?"

Angel released Leilani.

She leaped to her feet and helped others up from the pile of people on the floor.

Josh scrambled down the ladder, grabbed a snorkel and mask and jumped over the boat's port side.

Leilani and Angel leaned over the rail and watched the young deckhand swim along the hull, diving down several times along the length before reaching the bow. When he came up this time, he looked up to the top deck and called out, "The hull's damaged, but I think we can make it back to the harbor."

"Come aboard," the captain said. "Let's get this bucket moving." He turned to Leilani. "I contacted the Coast Guard. They're sending out a cutter to follow us in. The fire department has been alerted. They're sending people to help those injured. They'll be there when we get to the harbor. And our sister boat, the Windsong II, isn't far behind us. If we run into trouble before we get back, we can transfer passengers to the Windsong II or the Coast Guard cutter if it gets here before we make it back to Maalaea Harbor."

Leilani nodded and turned to the passengers.

"Is our boat sinking?" a woman asked.

Leilani tilted her head, her brow pinching. "Yes and no. There is damage to the hull. Like Josh informed us, it's not bad enough to abandon ship. And you heard the captain. We have backup and backup for our backup. But I have faith in Windsong I. It will get us back to the harbor, no problem."

Angel could tell by her slightly strained tone that Leilani was worried but putting on a brave face for the people on board. She wouldn't let anything happen to them if she could help it. Unfortunately, shit happened. A lot of shit had happened to Leilani lately.

Angel's fists tightened. It was time to clean it up. He just needed a lead to chase.

Josh swam to the back of the boat.

Angel rushed to meet him, lowering the ladder. Josh climbed up several steps. When Angel reached out a hand, Josh grabbed hold.

Angel hauled him aboard and secured the ladder.

Captain Ako set the boat in motion, pushing it as fast as it could, which was sluggish at best.

"It's taking on water," Leilani whispered, her brow knit, her gaze tracking their progress as if gauging how far they might get before they had to transfer over to another craft.

Angel slipped his arm around her waist and pulled her against his side. "We'll make it back to the harbor."

"I hope so." Leilani sighed and turned back to the frightened passengers, forcing a smile on her face. "Everybody okay?"

A few had scrapes and bruises, but, for the most part, they were okay.

Their happy chatter from before the crash had faded into silence, with only a few whispers exchanged to calm a child or a nervous female.

Leilani went from person to person with her clipboard, making notes about each guest's injuries.

Angel followed with the first aid kit, applying antibiotic ointment and bandages where needed.

"If any of you feel the need to go to a hospital, the

captain has relayed a message to the island's first responders," Leilani said. "An ambulance should be waiting for us when we arrive at Maalaea Harbor. For anything the emergency medical technicians can't fix with a bandage, you can have the ambulance take you to the emergency room where a doctor can check you over."

Although some wanted an EMT to check them out and treat their scrapes, no one proclaimed a need for an ambulance.

"If you've hit your head at all, you should go to the hospital and have them check you out," she urged. "You could have a concussion."

When the harbor came into view, Angel could see the tension ease out of Leilani's shoulders. The Windsong I was still moving forward. The Windsong II had caught up, and the Coast Guard cutter was just now coming into view.

With a few more minutes yet to go, Leilani stood in the middle of the passengers. "I'm so sorry your amazing trip ended the way it did. If you want a refund, contact me, and I'll do my best to process the refunds in a timely manner." She gave them a weak smile. "I'm so sorry this happened. I hope it doesn't ruin your enjoyment of the remainder of your stay on Maui."

Angel could listen to Leilani's soft tones all day, every day. She had a way of making people calm.

"Don't let the actions of one nutjob taint your

opinion of Maui." Leilani looked around at all of the guests, a tight smile firmly affixed on her mouth. "Thank you for choosing Windsong Tours. We hope to see you again." Her lips twisted. "Of course, after we find out who attacked our boat and impound what's left of his boat."

"You go, girl!" a woman called out. "I don't need my money back from this tour. You and your crew worked hard to make our adventure fun and informative. It wasn't your fault that a crazy boat driver ran into our boat."

"We hope the damage is easily fixed and the Windsong I is back up and touring in no time," an older gentleman said. "Thank you for the adventure."

Leilani's eyes glazed with tears. "Thanks, all of you, for your support. Please, enjoy the rest of your stay on Maui."

The closer they got to the harbor, the slower the Windsong I became until the captain made the command decision to ease into the nearest slip that would fit the big boat rather than limp to its assigned slot.

As soon as the boat came to a halt, Josh and Angel sprang into action, getting the steps situated so that the passengers could easily walk out of the boat onto the dock.

With Angel on one side and Josh on the other, they assisted everyone onto the dock to ensure no further injuries occurred.

Once they were off the dock and firmly on shore, the EMTs circulated among them, checking them for more serious injuries. Most were cleared to leave, but a few were detained while having minor scrapes cleaned and bandaged.

While the guests were being evaluated, an officer from the Maui Police Department approached Leilani. "We were notified that there was a hit-and-run incident on the water involving a jet boat and your vessel."

Leilani's lips thinned. "That's right."

Angel stood beside her, a hand at the small of her back, letting her know she wasn't alone.

Leilani filled in the officer on what had occurred as the man took notes on an electronic pad.

Angel gave his account as well, describing the boat. "It was black with red-orange flames on the side."

"Did you see the driver?" the officer asked.

Angel shook his head. It had happened so fast, and they'd had to brace for impact. "No. Whoever it was driving was riding low at the helm. As much damage as the jet boat caused to Ms. Kealoha's boat, the crash had to have caused significant damage to the jet boat. Find a boat with a damaged starboard side, and you'll know it was the one used to ram the Windsong I."

The officer nodded. "We'll release a BOLO, be on the lookout, for a jet boat matching your description," the officer promised. "We'll have our officers check harbors and marinas. Let us know if you think of anything else."

Before he left, the officer spoke to a few of the passengers, then Captain Ako and Josh.

Captain Ako arranged to have the Windsong I moved to a repair shop as soon as possible. He emphasized the fact it was taking on water and needed to be moved for repair before it sank. If they didn't move it soon, they might have to send a salvage team to recover it from the bottom of the harbor.

By then, the Windsong II had docked, and the guests had disembarked.

Leilani met with Captain Ako, Captain Dave and the deckhands.

"Up until today, the attacks have been passive, when no passengers or members of the crew were around." Her lips pressed into a tight line. "Today's incident changed all that. Whoever has been sabotaging our tour operation upped the stakes by attacking a boat full of people. Today's incident could've ended much more tragically than it did. People could've been seriously injured or killed." She shook her head. "I'm considering suspending operations until we get to the bottom of this. For now, we'll finish out this week's Windsong II reservations with eyes wide open to danger."

The captains and deckhands nodded as one, the

repercussions of shutting down the tours reflected in their grim expressions.

"If we do suspend operations, you know I'd like to pay you while we're down, but I can't," Leilani said. "Without the money from the tours coming in, I have nothing to fund salaries. I'll pay you up through the end of the week. As much as I hate it, I realize you have to go where you can make money. I hope I can hire you back when this is over, but I'll understand if you've found a better position. I'm sorry, but I'd rather lose you to a competitor than lose you forever."

"Well," Captain Dave said, "we have until the end of the week to figure it out. If any of you hear anything, let me or Leilani know."

"That's right," Leilani agreed. "We can't sit on information, no matter how big or small it might appear. One little nugget of data could mean the difference between taking a month to figure this out and resolving it within days, hours or even minutes."

"What about the Windsong II?" Dev asked. "You still need me to pull guard duty overnight?"

Leilani nodded. "More than ever. Windsong I will be in the maintenance building where they have video surveillance. I'll still need people to guard Windsong II, twenty-four-seven."

Dev nodded. "Between Reid and I, we can alternate night and day shifts to keep it covered."

"Great," Leilani said. "Then you won't be so tired because you were up all night and the following day."

"We'll work it out so that neither one of us will have to work it twenty-four-seven," Dev assured her.

One by one, she hugged each one of the captains and deckhands and asked them to give her love to their family members.

"Thank you," Leilani said and turned to Angel. "Now, can we go home? I'm beyond exhausted, and I have some things I need to do for my cousin's wedding." She shook her head. "It all seems so inconsequential compared to nearly losing my crew, a boat and all its passengers."

"Yeah, but he's your cousin," Angel said.

Leilani nodded. "He's already lost so much and postponed their wedding once. My problems aren't his. I need to keep it that way."

"Come on," Angel said. "I'll get you back to the resort. After a shower and change of clothes, you'll feel more like dealing with the wedding."

"I hope so." She followed him to his rental car and let him open the door for her.

Angel waited until Leilani was settled in the passenger seat before he rounded the front of the car and slid behind the wheel.

She held out her hand.

He took it in his and squeezed gently. "It's going to be okay."

She met his gaze. "Before or after someone's hurt?"

CHAPTER 8

"Preferably before." Angel released her hand, started the car and shifted into drive. "I'll check with our computer guy, Swede, and see if he has come up with anything in his research."

"I should skip the bridesmaids' dress fitting this afternoon. My time would be better spent talking to prime suspects. I can't have this happen again. Those people on board could've died." Leilani buried her face in her hands. "When that boat hit, all the guests on board were tossed like rag dolls. I'm surprised there weren't more injuries."

"Getting them on the floor helped. That was a brilliant move."

She snorted. "I really should shut down the tour business. It's selfish of me to keep going when there's so much potential for danger."

"We'll know to carry weapons next time. If someone comes at us like the jet boat did today, we can open fire."

Leilani's stomach dropped at the thought. "What if they shoot back?" She threw up her hands. "Then we could have bullet wounds along with the bruises, scrapes and concussions from having our boat rammed. And don't forget the potential for capsizing and drowning." She leaned her head against the seat and closed her eyes. "I should cancel tomorrow's snorkeling trip."

Angel lifted her hand in his, glanced briefly toward her and then returned his attention to the road. "I doubt you'll have another boat attack," he said, "but now that I voiced that prediction, we probably will." He grimaced in her direction. "I'd knock on wood, but there's not much wood in modern vehicles."

"Why?" she said, gulping back the sob rising up her throat.

"Why don't they put wood trim in cars like they used to?" he shook his head. "Beats me."

She laughed, the sound choked by the lump lodged around her vocal cords. "Why are they attacking my business?"

Angel's brow dipped. "I don't know. Hopefully, they'll find the boat and whoever drove it into the Windsong. Until they do, we have little to go on."

"So, we keep operating what we have left until the next thing happens?" She shook her head. "The fires were bad enough. We haven't even recovered from them. Now this. I could handle all of it if it was just me they were targeting. But it's not just me."

She pushed the stray hairs back from her face. "My crews are like family. I got the tour company back up and running as soon as I could so they would have a way to make a living. Attacking the boat was an attack on the company and my crew family. And God bless the people who put their trust in our hands to take their loved ones on a safe excursion." She looked at the road ahead. "There has to be something I can do to make this stop."

"And that might be the motivation behind the attacks."

"To make me stop the tours? To cut off any kind of income stream and leave me with only one option?" She drew in a breath and let it out slowly. "I'd have to sell the business and land I inherited from my father and grandfather."

"Which brings us back to the real estate brokers who've been hounding you to do just that," Angel said.

"I'm not the only landowner in Lahaina. I haven't heard of any of them being targeted like this." None of it made sense to Leilani.

He cast a glance her way. "Have you been in touch with any of the other landowners?"

"Some. The people who owned property on either side of mine. But it's been a few weeks. I should do that now." She pulled her cell phone out of her pocket and dialed the number for Celeste Romano, the woman who'd owned the clothing shop on the south side of Leilani's building. "Let's see what Celeste has to say."

Celeste answered on the second ring. "Leilani, how are you?"

"I'm okay," Leilani lied. "How about you? Are you still at the Westin?"

"I was until last week," her friend said. "I found a house to rent with a yard and access to the beach. The Westin was nice to let me stay with my dog, but I felt like we were overstaying our welcome, especially when they started filling up with paying customers. Having a big dog on the resort that normally doesn't allow pets was pushing their limits. Besides, Winston loves the house and walks along the beach. What about you? Still at the Palms?"

"I am."

"Did you get your tour business up and running in time for the reopening of Maui's tourism?" Celeste asked.

"I did," Leilani said. "How is your online store working out for you?"

"Better than I could've hoped for. I rented a storage unit to stage products and package shipments. I make enough to pay my bills and rent this house."

Leilani took a deep breath and jumped in. "Have you made any decisions on what you're going to do with your property in Lahaina?"

"I'm still on the fence. It's taking forever for the insurance company to give me numbers. Not that we could do anything with the insurance money until the cleanup efforts are complete. The best part about the online store is that I'm maintaining connections with my clothing distributors. That will make it easier for me when or if I set up my new brick-and-mortar store." She paused for only a second. "Are you being bombarded with calls and unsolicited visits from brokers making offers for your land?"

"Yes," Leilani sank back in her seat. "Every day. This morning, I had half a dozen of them at my door waving contracts. They gave me some story about receiving word from me that I was ready to sell. I never sent a message like that."

"Wow," Celeste said. "You're the last person I would ever expect to sell your property there. You always told me it was your last connection to your family. So, are you going to sell?"

"No," Leilani said. "I've told all of them the same thing, but they're persistent."

Celeste snorted. "I'd say they're relentless. I get several calls a day. I block the numbers, but they just use different numbers to call again. Can't say that they've come en masse to my door. That's kind of creepy."

"Real creepy," Leilani agreed.

"Although I have to admit, it would be easier to take the money and run. They've made some amazing offers. And selling would mean I could get on with my life *now* instead of waiting for Lahaina to open up and let us back in to rebuild. Just think, if you sold your place, you'd probably make enough that you wouldn't have to work another day in your life. You could paint full-time and live anywhere in the world."

Leilani had thought the same several times, wondering if it was really worth keeping the property. But she couldn't sell.

"Maui is my home," Leilani said softly.

Celeste sighed. "Yeah. That's the rub. It's in your blood, your heritage. I get that. And that's why I haven't sold my place. I love having a store on Front Street. We have the most beautiful view of the ocean and a close community of people I consider family."

"We *had* a close community," Leilani said. "We're scattered to the winds now."

"Do you think they'll come back?" Celeste asked. "Will we ever get back to normal?"

"I don't think so," Leilani said. "Some of us will return to Lahaina, but not all. New people will move in. It will be up to us natives to preserve our culture."

"You're right," Celeste said.

"Celeste," Leilani finally got to the reason for her call. "Have any of the brokers gotten pushy or heavy-handed in their methods to convince you to sell?"

"How do you mean?" Celeste asked.

"Have they done anything to scare you into moving off Maui? Have they impacted your online business in any way that would make you fail and be forced to sell your place in Lahaina to stay afloat?"

"No," Celeste said. "Why do you ask? Are they harassing you with more than phone calls and showing up on your doorstep?"

"Maybe."

"Spill, girl," Celeste said. "You can't start a conversation like that and leave me hanging."

Leilani told her friend about the diesel in the boat tanks, the slashed tires and ended with the boat attack that day.

"Oh my god, Leilani," Celeste exclaimed. "Nothing like that has happened to me. Are you sure it's the brokers doing it? I mean, my property is right next to yours. If they're so rabid to get yours, wouldn't they want mine, too?"

"That's just it." Leilani sighed. "Who else would attack my business?"

"Your competitors? Although why they'd start now is beyond me. Are you the only tour company being targeted?"

"That I know of," Leilani answered. "But why

would they target me now? Why not before the fires?"

"So many people who worked in the service industry have left the island. Are you competing for the people you need to operate the tours?"

"We're operating on a skeletal staff. I've been filling in where I can. But that's just a handful of people. Why destroy a business for a handful of people?"

"Do you have a crazy ex-boyfriend I don't know about?" Celeste laughed. "No, it can't be that. You haven't been on a date in over a year. Unless you found one recently. Have you?"

Leilani shot a glance toward Angel as he pulled through the gate to the resort. "No. I haven't." But she was open to the possibility with the man beside her.

"Then I can't imagine who would do this to your business. It's like they're trying to shut you down." Celeste paused. "What about the people who don't want tourism to return to Maui?"

"I'm looking at all possibilities. They came to mind. I just don't think they would resort to violence to stop tourism from returning to the island. And, again, why just my company?"

"You have me stumped," Celeste said. "I haven't experienced what you're going through. I'm sorry you are. If there's anything I can do to help, please don't hesitate to ask. Do you need Winston to come stay with you for protection?"

"No, thank you." Leilani smiled at the memory of the big Goldendoodle lying across the floor of Celeste's clothing store, soaking up the sun. "Though I love him, he's happiest with you."

"Hey, did your cousin and his fiancée ever get married?" Celeste asked.

"Not yet," Leilani said. "They found a new venue and set the date for a month from now."

"How's he doing since the fire?" Celeste asked.

"Good. He's living at the resort where he works."

"Are he and his fiancée still surfing competitively?"

"I think they're working up to it again. They had to order new boards since their competition boards were in the house they were renovating. They lost everything they owned."

"Didn't we all?" Celeste said softly. "I hope you find out what's going on soon. If you need a place to stay, I have a spare bedroom. Winston would love having you around. He misses you. Hell, I miss you."

"I miss you, too, Celeste. Let's talk soon." As Leilani ended the call, Angel was pulling into a parking space.

He shifted into park and turned off the engine.

Leilani sat for a moment longer, digesting her conversation. "Celeste owned the store next to mine. She's getting calls from brokers, but no attacks."

"It's just you, then?"

"I still need to call Larry Fenton. He owned the souvenir shop on the other end of my building."

"Do it," Angel said. "Call him."

"I need to get a shower and get ready to go to a dress fitting with my future cousin-in-law's bridesmaids."

"Then make it a quick call," Angel said.

Leilani looked up Larry's number and called.

"This is Larry," he answered.

Five minutes later, she ended the call, shaking her head. "Larry is getting calls, but no attacks." She pushed the car door open and got out.

Angel came around the front of the vehicle and walked with her toward her section of the resort. "Is your building larger than Celeste's or Larry's?"

Leilani nodded. "I had three shops, each equal in size to Celeste's and Larry's. And I had parking behind mine."

Angel's eyes narrowed. "Could it be whoever is harassing you is trying to get you to sell first, with the idea that once you do, the others will fall in line?"

"It's possible," Leilani said. "Celeste and Larry aren't native Hawaiians. They don't feel as rooted in Maui as I do. My family has been here for centuries. Celeste came to Maui twenty years ago to visit and never left. Larry's father retired from the military on Oahu. Larry moved to Maui when he got tired of the traffic in Honolulu." She shrugged. "It just seems like a lot of effort to get me to sell. Plus, what big corporation would risk getting caught sabotaging a small business?"

Angel tipped his head toward her, his lips twisting. "A corporation with a lot of money and a team of attorneys who could get them out of anything."

Leilani sighed. "I guess it could happen." She stopped in front of her door and faced Angel. "Will I see you later?" How was that for being ballsy? She held her breath, afraid she was being too pushy. But, boy, she wanted to see him again.

He grasped both of her hands. "Where you go, I go. If I'm to protect you, I need to be with you."

Her heart fluttered. "I thought you were protecting my business."

He shook his head. "You are your business. You were guiding the tour yesterday when they slashed your tires. You were on the boat that was hit today. Were you on the boat they poured diesel into?"

Leilani thought back, her brow twisting, "Yes, I was."

"Seems to me they're targeting your business and maybe more specifically you."

A chill rippled down the back of Leilani's neck. "That's not reassuring."

"And that's why I've now become your shadow. Where you go, I go." He tipped her chin up. "Starting tonight, I'll camp outside your door."

"I have a couch in my suite," she offered, her voice

breathless, butterflies battering the inside of her belly.

His lips twitched. "Only if you're okay with a strange man sleeping in the same suite with you."

She nodded, her thoughts zooming ahead to the night and all the possibilities. "Do you really think someone would try to attack me here at the resort?"

"Did you think someone would attack you on the boat?" he countered.

Her gut clenched. "No."

CHAPTER 9

STILL HOLDING LEILANI'S HANDS, Angel captured and held her gaze. "Twenty-four-seven, Leilani. I can't protect you if I'm not with you twenty-four-seven."

Leilani's pulse leaped. "Even my bridesmaids' dress fitting?"

His lips twitched. "Even your fitting." His nose wrinkled. "We both need to shower before we do anything."

Leilani's instinct was to offer to let him shower with her. She opened her mouth to say that, but he beat her to the punch.

"I'm going to leave you for just a few minutes. While I'm gone, I want you to stay in your suite with the door locked." He let go of one of her hands. "Your key?"

She fished in her pocket for the key and handed it to him. Was she insane, giving him the key to her

134

room? A stranger she'd only known a little more than a day.

He waved the key over the lock. When the light turned green, he opened the door, stepped inside, pulled her through and closed the door behind her. "Let me clear the suite before you go any further."

She frowned. "Is that necessary? The door locks when I leave."

"Humor me?" he said.

Leilani waved a hand at the interior. "Knock yourself out."

As he moved about the suite, she cringed, wishing she'd taken a little more time to straighten and organize the items she'd accumulated over the past few months. When he stepped into the bedroom, she tried to visualize how she'd left it that morning. Had she made the bed and picked up the dirty laundry?

She made a note to herself to make more of an effort to tidy up before leaving her place each day. She never knew when she might entertain a handsome male guest.

Leilani chuckled. She hadn't entertained a male guest in a very long time. Why would she have thought it would happen today?

"All clear." Angel emerged from her bedroom. When he saw her, he frowned. "What's so funny?"

She smiled. "Nothing. It just seems like a bit of overkill."

"I might have agreed with you yesterday," he said.

"But the attack today was violent and potentially deadly. If the person who was driving that boat had the balls to attack a boatload of people, he might consider one lone female to be easy pickings."

Leilani shivered. "If you're trying to scare me, you're doing a good job."

"Good." He tucked a strand of her hair behind her ear. "Better scared than dead."

Sparks of electricity ignited her nerves where his fingers brushed her cheek and ear.

"You'd better hurry through the shower. I'll hit the shower in my room, grab my things and be back before you're done." Angel held up her key. "Mind if I hold onto this to let myself in if you're still in the bathroom?"

She shook her head. "Please do." *And join me in the shower*, she wanted to add but bit down on her tongue to keep from blurting it out.

He stared at her a moment longer as if he wanted to say something else but must have thought better of it. He stepped around her and hurried out the door, closing it firmly behind him.

Leilani followed and stood in front of the closed door. She peeked through the peephole, watching him jog toward the building where his room was located.

At the rate he was moving, he'd be back before she had a chance to get in the shower.

Leilani spun and raced for the bathroom, stripping off her clothes as she went. She didn't even wait for the water to warm before she stepped beneath it and gasped. "Holy hell," she muttered, reaching for the bottle of body wash. With a loofa, she scrubbed the salt from her skin and then poured shampoo into her palm.

After washing the salt from her long hair, she rinsed it thoroughly and applied a healthy amount of conditioner. Every time she went out on the boat, she always returned with her hair a tangled mess no brush could penetrate until she washed it and treated it with conditioner. She ran her brush through her hair while the conditioner was still in it to free the tangles caused by the salt water and wind. When she had all the knots out, she rinsed from head to toe and turned off the water.

She stood for a moment, listening for sounds of movement from the other room. When she didn't hear any, she quickly dried her body and wrapped her wet hair in the towel. She didn't have time to dry her hair before she had to leave for the fitting, but the towel would absorb sufficient moisture so that her hair wouldn't drip down her back.

Still naked, Leilani dashed into the bedroom and grabbed white panties, a strapless bra and the pale blue sundress she'd ordered online so that she'd have a dress to wear for this fitting and the rehearsal dinner. Back in the bathroom, she was just closing the door when she heard the sound of the suite door opening and closing.

"I'm back," Angel called out, his voice muffled by the bedroom door.

"I'll be ready in a few minutes," she responded as she stepped into the panties. The silky fabric gliding up her legs made her think of Angel's fingers caressing her there. Her entire body warmed at the idea, heat flowing through her veins to coil at her center.

"Chill, Lani," she said to the woman in the mirror. "He's here to protect you, not make love to you."

"Did you say something," Angel asked.

"Just singing to myself," Leilani called out. Then she muttered beneath her breath, "Wishful thinking."

After she finished dressing, she applied a little blush to her cheeks, a thin streak of eyeliner and a quick brush of mascara. Her dark skin didn't need much. It glowed naturally, a gift of her heritage. Leilani added a dash of gloss to her lips and brushed her damp hair straight back from her forehead. Already, wispy tendrils were drying into long curls.

As she passed through the bedroom, she slid her feet into a pair of strappy sandals and pulled open the door. "I'm ready."

Angel turned from where he stood by the window. He wore navy slacks and a sky-blue polo shirt. He'd slicked his damp hair back from his forehead, but he hadn't shaved, leaving a sexy dark shadow of a beard on his chin and jaw.

His gaze swept over her like a caress. "You look amazing."

Leilani's cheeks warmed. "Thanks. My car or yours?"

"Mine," he said. "Might as well put the miles on the rental. And leave yours here for Olina to use if she needs it."

"I'll let her know to keep the keys," Leilani said.

He opened the door, looked out at the surroundings then held the door for her.

Leilani stepped out onto the porch and turned toward Olina's door.

She had just raised her hand to knock when Olina opened the door.

"Oh," her friend said. "I was just about to come to your place to give you the keys to the car." Her gaze went to the man behind her. "Are you going somewhere?"

Leilani nodded. "I have the dress fitting with the bridesmaids for Makai's wedding."

"Oh, then you'll need these." Olina held out the key fob.

Leilani shook her head. "I was just coming over to tell you to keep them tonight. Angel is taking me in his car. I won't need mine."

"Okay." She smiled. "Thanks."

Noa slipped through the gap between his mother

and the door and stared up at Leilani. "Lani, you look like a princess."

Leilani bent to lift the little boy into her arms.

He hugged her around her neck and said, "You smell good."

Leilani laughed. "Thank you."

He leaned back and stared into her eyes. "Will you read us a story?"

Leilani sighed. "I'm sorry, Noa. I have to go somewhere." She kissed his cheek and set him back on his feet. "Maybe Mamo will read to you."

"I like it when you read." Noa looked past Leilani to Angel and frowned. "Who is that man?"

Leilani had to hide a smile at the suspicious glance Noa gave Angel. "This is my friend Angelo." She hooked Angel's arm and drew him forward. "Angel, this is Noa."

Angel knelt on one knee in front of the little boy and held out his hand. "Hi, Noa. It's nice to meet you."

Noa took his hand, his frown deepening. "Are you going to marry my Lani?"

"I don't know," Angel said. "She's a princess, but I'm not a prince. Is it allowed?"

Noa tilted his head. "If the princess loves you with her whole heart, I think it's okay." He looked to Leilani. "Do you love him with your whole heart?"

Heat burned in Leilani's cheeks. "I don't know, Noa. We only met yesterday."

He looked from Leilani back to Angel. "If you want her to fall in love with you, she likes flowers."

Angel nodded, his face serious. "Thank you for the tip."

Noa leaned toward Angel and cupped his hand around the man's ear. "Even more than flowers, she likes paintbrushes."

Though the boy whispered, Leilani heard what he said, and her heart melted. Noa might be a little guy, but he paid attention to the people around him, especially the ones he loved.

"I'll keep that in mind," Angel said, holding out his fist.

Noa bumped his fist against Angel's. "Nice to meet you, Mr. Angelo." The boy looked at Leilani once more and then ducked past his mother's legs into the suite.

Olina grinned. "I never know what's going to come out of that boy's mouth." She glanced over her shoulder into the room behind her and then back at Leilani. "He's got a big heart and loves his Lani."

"I love him, too," Leilani said.

Olina's smile slipped away. "I heard what happened on your tour today. I'm glad no one was hurt badly. It blows my mind that someone would purposely ram into your boat."

"Blows my mind, too."

"Be careful, Lani," Olina said. "We love you."

Leilani hugged her friend. "I love you, too. I'll be all right. I've got to go, or I'll be late."

Angel guided her to his car and held the door while she settled in the passenger seat.

Once he got in, she gave him directions to the Bridal Boutique from Alyssa's texted invitation. Alyssa had given their sizes to the boutique and had the staff order matching dresses in pastel peach to compliment the colors that would be in Alyssa's bridal bouquet. They were to meet at the boutique to try on the dresses and have them fitted by a seamstress.

They drove from the resort across the island to Kahului, arriving at the boutique five minutes before five o'clock, the time Alyssa had reserved.

Leilani frowned and glanced down at her phone, pulling up Alyssa's last text with the date, time and location of the fitting.

"Are you sure this is the place?" Angel asked.

She held out her phone. "It's what she texted to me two weeks ago."

He looked at the text and at the building. "The sign on the door reads CLOSED."

Leilani called Alyssa's number. The phone rang six times before her voicemail picked up.

"Alyssa, it's Leilani. I'm at the boutique you listed in your text message, and no one is here. Was the time, date or location changed? Call me when you get this message." She ended the call and dialed her cousin.

Makai answered on the second ring. "Hey, Leilani, I can't speak now. I'm in the middle of something for work."

"Real quick, do you know where Alyssa is meeting her bridesmaids for their fittings?"

"No clue," he responded. "Call her. I have to go." He ended the call before Leilani could tell him that she had tried to call his fiancée, but she didn't pick up.

"He didn't know?" Angel asked.

Leilani shook her head, frowning.

"Can you call one of the other bridesmaids?" Angel asked.

"I'm not sure I have their numbers." She pulled up her contacts list and scrolled through, looking for the maid of honor, Brooke Owens. Thankfully, she found her and called her number.

After the fourth ring, Leilani was about to give up when Brooke answered, "Hello. This is Brooke."

"Brooke, it's Leilani, Makai's cousin."

"Leilani, we were just talking about you, wondering where you were. We thought you said you were coming to the fitting."

"I'm here now at the Bridal Boutique," Leilani said.

"But that's not where it is. We're at my parent's house. The boutique sent the dresses and their seamstress here for a more intimate setting. Since Alyssa sent out the original invitation, I thought she let everyone know the location had changed."

"I didn't get the message," Leilani said, careful not to let her irritation come across in her tone.

"Hold on, I'll text you the address. When you get to the gate, just hit the call button, and I'll let the gate guard know to let you in. Don't worry about being late. Alyssa is running behind as well. See you in a few."

Brooke ended the call before Leilani could tell her that she was bringing Angel with her. Her lips pressed together. Well, Angel would just have to be a surprise, and they'd have to be okay with that, or Leilani would go back to the resort, pop open a bottle of wine and not give a damn what the other bridesmaids thought.

She really would rather go back to the resort and drink wine anyway.

Then she thought about Makai and the fact that she was his only living relative. He'd wanted her to be in his wedding. Leilani suspected Alyssa had felt obligated to invite her to be one of her bridesmaids.

Her phone pinged with the incoming text from Brooke with the address of her parent's home.

Leilani brought it up on her map.

"Is that the new location of the fitting?" Angel asked, pulling out of the parking lot.

Leilani nodded. "Everyone else got the message

but me. But Brooke says it's okay because the bride is running late anyway." She shot an apologetic glance toward Angel. "I'm sorry you're getting dragged around. I can think of a dozen other things I'd rather be doing. I can imagine you're feeling the same."

He smiled. "It's okay. I'm in good company. I can't complain."

His words made her feel only slightly better. She still had to get through an evening with a gaggle of women who were Alyssa's friends, not hers. Leilani was the odd man out—the obligatory family member.

She reminded herself she was doing this for her cousin. Squaring her shoulders, she was determined not to be the Debbie Downer of the party.

They drove another twenty minutes to a gated community in the hills, stopping at the gate where Angel gave Leilani's name to the gate guard. The man checked his list, nodded and punched a button, raising the gate bar.

Angel drove through, following the GPS through winding streets and coming to a stop on a hill in front of a large stucco house with massive picture windows and views of the Pacific Ocean in the distance. He parked to the side of the house, next to a line of sports cars.

Angel got out of the car and came around to open Leilani's door. "Does your cousin's fiancée come from a wealthy family?"

Leilani shook her head. "Not at all. Though I

think she attended a private school on scholarship because of her prowess at surfing. She's won a few competitions in her class. Makai told me that she's been scouted by some companies that want her to represent their brand of beachwear and surfing gear."

"She's that good?" Angel asked as they walked toward the front door.

"That's how she and Makai met, at surfing competitions. They're both highly competitive. Or at least, they were before the fires. They haven't been to a competition since because they were waiting on special boards to replace the ones they lost."

At the door, Angel rang the bell.

A pretty young woman with perfectly styled, bleached-blond hair pulled the door open.

"Leilani," she said. "I'm glad you finally made it."

Leilani gave Brook a tight smile. "Me, too. Sorry I'm late."

"It's okay. We started the party without you. The seamstress should be ready for you next." Brooke looked from Leilani to Angel and gave him a sultry smile. "And who is the delicious man with you?"

Leilani gritted her teeth and clenched her fists. She didn't like the way Brooke was running her gaze over Angel or the sexy voice she'd used on him.

"Brooke," she said tightly. "This is—"

"Angelo." Angel smiled and held out a hand. "I'm Leilani's boyfriend."

Leilani fought to hide her shock at Angel's

announcement. It helped to see Brooke's sexy smile fade to disappointment.

Take that, bitch.

Leilani smiled up at Angel. "I hope you don't mind that I brought him. I loaned my car to a friend in need."

"No, it's quite all right." Brooke backed into the foyer, holding the door wide. "Please, come in. The girls are in the formal living room getting pinned. Alyssa called a few minutes ago. She'll be here in five minutes. An errand she had to run took longer than she expected."

She led the way into a formal living room with ultra-modern, white leather sectional sofas, glass and stone accent pieces and multifaceted chandeliers raining light onto the occupants.

Six bridesmaids stood around the room, wearing the peach dresses in various stages of being pinned for alterations.

The woman with the pincushion attached to her wrist like a bracelet handed a dress to Leilani with a frown. "You're much smaller than the size I was given," she said as if it was Leilani's fault that she'd ordered the wrong dress size. "We'll have to see if we can alter it enough to fit without taking it completely apart and starting over."

Brooke laughed. "Don't mind Susan; she's just getting tired after fitting all of us. You can change in the powder room down the hall, first door on the right."

When Leilani moved toward the hallway, Angel followed.

Brooke stepped between them. "Why don't you have a seat while she's getting dressed? Can I get you a drink?"

Angel's gaze met Leilani's over Brooke's shoulder.

"Get comfortable," Leilani said. "I'll be right back." She almost smiled as he frowned, clearly unhappy about being trapped in the room full of women.

Leilani hurried to the bathroom, unwilling to leave him alone with Brooke for longer than necessary.

In record time, she flew out of her dress and into the one she'd been handed, only to discover the garment was four times too large on her petite frame. It hung like a loose moo-moo, exposing more of her body than she liked without the advantage of a bikini beneath it.

Wrapping her arms over her chest to keep the neckline from draping down to her belly button, she left the bathroom and hurried back to the formal living room.

When she entered, all gazes turned to her. The other bridesmaids snickered.

Angel sat in a corner chair, a glass of whiskey in his hand, his gaze meeting Leilani's, a slight frown denting his forehead. He mouthed the words, *Are you all right?*

Leilani's heart warmed at his concern. She gave a brief nod, crossed to where he sat and handed her cell phone to him.

Susan, the seamstress, clucked her tongue and advanced on Leilani, shaking her head. She grabbed a handful of fabric at the back of the gown and pulled tight. Using a set of large fabric clamps she secure the clump of fabric in place.

Leilani was able to lower her arms without embarrassing herself in front of Angel and the others.

Working quickly and efficiently, Susan pinned the gown to fit Leilani's small waist, the swell of her breasts and hips and brought the hem up eight inches.

The poor woman would have her hands full, reworking the dress for Leilani.

By the time she'd finished, Leilani couldn't move without being stuck by a pin.

"You can change back into your clothes," Susan said. "Be careful not to lose any pins."

"Yes, ma'am," Leilani hurried to the bathroom and changed back into the pretty blue dress that fit her body so much better than the peach gown.

When she returned to the living room, Alyssa had arrived and was surrounded by her bridesmaids, who were all talking at once.

Leilani handed the pinned gown to Susan with an apologetic smile. "Good luck," she said softly.

"Leilani," Alyssa exclaimed. "There you are. For a moment, I thought you'd forgotten about the fitting."

Leilani fought the urge to point out the fact that Alyssa hadn't told her the fitting had been moved to Brooke's parent's house. Instead, she forced a smile. "I didn't forget. I was changing."

Alyssa brushed her long blond hair over her shoulder, shifting the swath of hair hanging low over her forehead.

Brooke gasped. "Alyssa, what happened to your forehead?"

Alyssa touched a finger to the small cut and bruise there. "Nothing much. I was testing my new board and got tossed by a wave. The board bounced back and hit me."

"Oh, Alyssa, honey," Brooke said. "Come and sit." She led Alyssa to the white leather sectional and pressed her into the seat. "I'll get you a drink." She hurried to the bar and poured champagne into a flute. When she returned to hand the glass to Alyssa, she said. "You need to be more careful. You could've been hurt badly, even knocked out."

Alyssa laughed. "Really, it's nothing. I've had worse. It's all part of being a professional surfer."

"You're so brave," one of the other bridesmaids said. "Those big waves scare me."

Alyssa smiled. "I love what I do. I can't imagine doing anything else."

"Are you still working at the resort?" Brooke asked.

"Sadly, yes." Alyssa sipped the champagne.

Brooke lifted another glass of champagne from one of the glass side tables and sat beside Alyssa. "I thought you were going to quit."

Her lips firmed into a straight line. "I would have had I gotten the endorsement contract from Billabong."

"That was so disappointing," Brooke said. "You'd think they would have waited for the smoke to clear, so to speak."

Leilani winced at Brooke's flippant reference to the fires that had killed a hundred people and left so many more homeless, including Alyssa and Makai.

"It's okay," Alyssa said. "I've got other opportunities in the works."

A bridesmaid clapped her hands together. "Another competition?"

"Among other things, Makai and I have our names in the hat for the Eddie," Alyssa said. "They think it'll run in January this year."

All eyes widened.

"Do you think you'll get an invitation?" Brooke asked. "Isn't it hard to get one?"

Alyssa nodded. "We've been training hard and

have placed in other competitions. I think we have a real chance."

"But your wedding is at the end of January," Leilani said. "Will the competition interfere with your nuptials?"

Alyssa shook her head. "I don't think so. Don't worry. This wedding has been delayed once. I won't let it be delayed again. Makai and I are a team. I can't wait to marry him." Alyssa held up her champagne glass. "Enough talk about surfing. We're here to get ready for a wedding."

"Your wedding," Brooke said. "To the bride and groom!"

The other ladies grabbed their champagne glasses and raised them in the air.

Angel placed his whiskey glass in Leilani's empty hand.

She gave him a grateful smile and lifted the glass to the bride and groom. "To the bride and groom."

Leilani stayed another ten minutes before she thanked Brooke for hosting and gave her future cousin-in-law a hug. "I'm happy for you and Makai, and I'm glad the insurance company came through so quickly so that you could get new boards and get out there to practice."

"Oh, I wish we had our insurance settlement already. We couldn't wait that long."

"But your new boards. How—"

Alyssa grimaced. "We maxed out our credit cards

on boards and deposits on the wedding venue, banking on the insurance claim going through soon."

Leilani winced. "Ouch."

Alyssa shrugged. "Things are going to work out."

Leilani smiled. "I'm sure they will."

She left with Angel a few minutes later.

Once in his car, she leaned her head back in the seat and closed her eyes.

Angel started the car, backed out of the parking space and drove out of the gated subdivision onto the highway. The sun was sinking low in the sky, turning the clouds various shades of pink and purple.

"They want to surf the Eddie," Leilani said.

"The Eddie?" Angel asked.

"It's one of the biggest competitions in Hawaii. The waves can get as big as sixty feet."

"That's insane."

Leilani glanced across at Angel. "I mean, Makai and Alyssa are good. But the Eddie..." She shook her head.

A cell phone rang somewhere in the car. Leilani looked for hers, then realized she'd handed it to Angel earlier.

He reached into his pocket and pulled out his cell phone. The ringing wasn't coming from it. Switching hands on the steering wheel, he reached into his other pocket, pulled out Leilani's cell phone and handed it to her.

The caller ID indicated the Maui Police Department. Her pulse quickening, she answered. "This is Leilani Kealoha."

"Ms. Kealoha, this is Detective Haddox with the Maui Police Department. We called to let you know a jet boat matching the description you gave the officer today was discovered floating off Ulua Beach this evening."

She leaned forward, her grip tightening on the cell phone. "Have you identified who it belongs to?"

"We have," Haddox said. "It belongs to Custom Charters out of Maalaea Harbor. When I paid their owner a visit, he didn't even know the boat was missing. It wasn't scheduled to be out today. None of his people took it out. They all have alibis putting them somewhere else besides in that boat. And they had witnesses to prove it. The owner concluded that the boat was stolen."

"Were you able to lift fingerprints?" she asked.

"We tried, but the steering wheel and anywhere someone might place his hands was wiped clean. We couldn't even get the prints of the owner or his staff. Whoever took the boat was careful not to leave a trace. We canvassed the area around the beach. No one saw the boat come ashore or anyone get out of it. A man walking his dog noticed it floating close to shore with no one on it and called it in."

Leilani's heart sank. "Thank you for letting me know."

"Sorry we don't have anything more definitive. We'll keep you informed of any new developments."

After the call ended, Leilani laid the phone in her lap.

"They found the boat," Angel said.

"Yes," she said. "It was stolen, wiped clean of fingerprints and no one saw anything when it was stolen out of Maalaea Harbor or abandoned off a beach." Leilani sighed. "I really was hoping the boat would give us a lead, not another dead end."

Angel reached across the console for her hand. "If he continues to pursue you and your business, he will screw up. We will find him."

Leilani's hands tightened into fists. "In the meantime, we live in fear of what he'll try next. I wish he'd come after me and leave my people alone. If he does, I'll be ready for him."

Angel squeezed her hand. "*We'll* be ready for him."

CHAPTER 10

THE SUN HAD SLIPPED below the horizon, taking its colorful hues with it. Stars appeared, dotting the sky with bright pinpoints of light.

Angel was pleased when, as soon as he helped Leilani out of the car, she tucked her hand in the crook of his arm. He liked having her close as they walked to her suite on the far side of the resort. It felt natural and relaxed, like they fit together.

Until they rounded a corner, and her building came into sight.

Leilani's hand tightened on his arm, and her body tensed beside him.

He looked down at her, a frown pulling at his brow. "What's wrong?"

"Nothing," she said a little too fast, as if she was nervous or scared.

"Look," he said. "If you're uncomfortable with me

staying in your suite, I really don't mind sleeping outside your door."

She glanced up at him, her eyes wide. "Why? Don't you want to sleep in my room? Do I make you uncomfortable?"

He chuckled. "Only in a good way," he admitted. Angel stopped walking and turned to face her. "I'm attracted to you. Sleeping in the room next to you will be..." his lips twisted as he searched for the right word, "challenging. But I promise I won't touch you." He shoved his hands into his pockets as if to prove his point as much to himself as to her. Inside, he was holding onto his control by a very thin thread. God, he wanted to reach out and pull her into his arms.

She looked up at him, starlight reflecting off her dark irises. Her arms wrapped around herself, and she trembled. "What if I want you to touch me?" she whispered.

The thread fraying, Angel pulled his hands from his pockets. "I promise not to touch you," he repeated, "unless...you want me to."

Leilani unwound her arms from around herself and placed her hands on his chest. "I want you to." This time, she didn't whisper. She spoke firmly, her gaze capturing and holding his.

"Are you sure?" he asked. "You've had a rough couple of days. I don't want to take advantage of you in a weak moment." He held up a hand. "Don't get me wrong, though. I've wanted to touch you since you landed in my lap on the waterfall trail."

She laughed. "And me at my most awkward." Leilani's mouth curved into a smile that spread across her face. She slipped her hand into his and led him to her suite. As she neared the door, she put a finger to her lips, motioning for him to be quiet, and pointed to the door next to hers.

He nodded, pulled her key card from his pocket and waved it over the door lock.

When the green light flashed, Leilani turned the handle and eased open the door.

Once they were both across the threshold, she closed the door softly behind them.

"Stay here," he whispered.

Her lips quirked, but she did as he said and waited for him to conduct his search of the living area, bedroom and bathroom. All the while, his pulse slammed through his veins, heat coiling in his groin. *Be cool,* he coached himself. *You're not a teenager with your first girl.*

He was back a moment later. Instead of taking it slowly and letting her set the pace, he scooped her up into his arms and carried her into the darkened bedroom. When he lowered her feet to the floor, she slid down the front of his body.

She had to know just how turned on he was as she skimmed over his engorged cock trapped behind the fly of his trousers.

Her eyes widened, and her cheeks flushed a soft pink beneath her darker skin tones. Her gaze met his. "It's been a while since I've slept with anyone," she whispered. "I'm not even sure I'm good at it."

"Don't over-think it," he said. "Just relax and let it happen." He bent and brushed his lips across hers, softly at first.

She lifted on her toes to deepen the kiss. When she opened to him, he swept in, claiming her tongue with his.

Angel's arms came up around her, crushing her to him, his control quickly slipping from his grasp.

His heart pounded against his chest, and his breathing grew erratic. Forced to come up for air, he used that moment to remind himself not to scare her. Their first time together should be at her pace, not at the insane pace the animal inside him would dictate.

He rested his forehead against hers and took several deep, steadying breaths.

While Angel regrouped, Leilani was full steam ahead. Her hands slipped over his shoulders and down his arms to his hands. She raised them, pressing them against her breasts.

Once he had a firm hold there, she tugged his polo shirt out of his waistband. Her fingers brushed across his skin, climbing up beneath his shirt, finding and tweaking his nipples.

Angel moaned and gently squeezed her breasts through the fabric of her dress.

Leilani captured his hands in hers and looked up into his eyes. "Too slow." Then she reached behind herself and pulled down the zipper on the back of her dress.

Angel brushed the thin straps over her shoulders.

The dress floated to the floor, a pool of blue fabric around her ankles.

Leilani stepped free and, once again, reached behind her. This time, she unhooked the strapless bra. It fell to the floor, freeing her breasts into Angel's hands.

She stood in a pair of lacy white panties and the strappy sandals, her long dark hair cascading in waves over her shoulders and down her back.

Naked looked natural on her, her exotic beauty all she needed.

"You're beautiful," he said.

Her eyes flared as she reached for the hem of his shirt and dragged it up his torso.

He took over, ripped it over his head and tossed it aside.

Leilani ran her hands over his chest, her fingers exploring the hard plains, angling downward to the waistband of his trousers. She unbuckled his belt, pulled it through the loops and tossed it onto a nearby chair. When she reached for the button on his fly, he covered her hands with his. "Wait."

Her brow furrowed.

Angel plucked his wallet out of his back pocket

and flipped it open. He breathed a sigh as he extracted the condom he kept there in case of an emergency. He had more in the duffel bag he'd brought with him earlier, but they were in the other room, and he didn't want to interrupt their progress and spoil the mood by calling a timeout.

"Perfect." Leilani plucked the condom from his fingers, tossed it onto the bed and went back to unbuttoning his trousers. When she pulled the zipper down, his cock sprang free into her hand.

She gasped. "Commando?"

"Sometimes," he admitted.

Her hand circled his length and pulled gently. "Had I known earlier, the fitting would've taken on an entirely different mood." With one hand holding his rod, she pushed his trousers down.

Angel toed off his shoes and kicked his pants to the side. Then he cupped her chin and bent to kiss her gently.

Her hand contracted around his dick as her tongue pushed past his teeth to caress his.

She broke the connection first. Her gaze locked with his as she sank to her knees. Then her focus shifted to her hand as she dragged it to the very tip of his cock and back down to the base, where she rolled his balls between her fingers.

Angel's breath caught, held and released as she repeated the process.

He fought to retain control, afraid he wouldn't last long if she kept doing what she was doing.

Then she took him into her mouth, her hands reaching around him. Her fingers dug into his buttocks and pulled him toward her, his cock sliding deeper until it bumped against the back of her throat.

She pushed him back until he was almost free, then pulled him back into the warmth of her mouth. Leilani set the pace, then let him take over with his own rhythm until he was pumping in and out, tension building, pushing him closer to the edge.

It felt good. Too good.

On the verge of orgasm, he pulled free, dragging in deep breaths, concentrating on not releasing. Not yet. He wanted her to feel as good as he did at that moment. He wanted to lead her to the very edge, then turn her inside out to the point she forgot everything bad that had happened and only lived in the moment.

Angel drew Leilani to her feet and walked her backward until she bumped into the bed and sat on the edge. He leaned over her, laying her back against the mattress and kissed her long and hard.

Then he moved from her mouth, trailing kisses across her cheek, over her chin and down the length of her throat. His hands moved lower, blazing the path his lips would follow, massaging her breasts, tweaking the nipples and moving on to allow his mouth to take over.

Angel captured a nipple between his teeth and rolled it gently, flicking the tip until it formed a tight little bead. He moved to the other and teased it as well, sucking it into his mouth, pulling gently until her back arched off the bed, pressing her breast deeper into his mouth.

His fingers skimmed across her belly, moving lower to the juncture of her thighs, curling into her to cup her sex and slip a finger into her slick channel. She was so wet.

His cock jerked in anticipation.

Angel moved down her body, dropping kisses against her soft skin.

He parted her knees and knelt on the floor between them, draping her legs over his shoulders.

With his thumbs, he parted her folds and blew a warm stream of air over her clit.

"Please," Leilani moaned, writhing against the mattress.

"Please stop?" he asked, his tongue snaking out to flick that nubbin.

"No," she gasped and leaned up on her elbows. "Don't stop. Please."

He chuckled and flicked her there again.

She dropped back on the mattress, her fingers curled into the comforter, and her hips rose, urging Angel to do it again.

He tapped his tongue against her clit, then swirled

it around the nubbin. At the same time, he slid two fingers into her channel.

Leilani's back arched off the mattress. She reached between her legs and wove her fingers into his hair, holding him down there as he relentlessly worked her clit with his tongue.

Leilani's raised her knees and rocked her hips in rhythm with his strokes. Soon, her body tensed, and she stopped moving.

Angel didn't let up. He'd brought her this far. He'd see her through to her release.

LEILANI'S BODY was so tight, so tense, teetering on the verge of something so exquisite she wanted to tip over the edge. At the same time, she wanted to revel in tantalizing anticipation.

Angel touched her like a master artist who applied his brush to a canvas with confidence, beauty and sheer strokes of genius. With each flick of his tongue, he layered more color and definition, building on his masterpiece, taking her on a journey to a cataclysmic crescendo like none she'd ever experienced.

The more he stroked, the more intense her composition became until one final flick set off an explosion that spewed every color of the rainbow to the stars.

Leilani soared on the waves of her release, her

body pulsing, quivering and rejoicing in its incredible intensity. When she came back to earth, the intensity had waned, replaced by her body's hunger for something more. The ache of an emptiness that needed to be filled.

She scooted back on the bed and then reached for Angel, urging him to rise over her, to fill the emptiness and complete what he'd started.

Angel climbed up her body and pressed his lips to hers, kissing her so gently it brought tears to Leilani's eyes. He rose to kneel between her legs, a frown denting his brow. "Where did it go?"

She stared up at him in an orgasm-induced haze. "Where did what go?"

His frown cleared. "There." Angel grabbed the packet Leilani had tossed on the bed a lifetime ago. In seconds, he had applied the condom and was back, leaning over her again.

"Hurry," she said, her channel still throbbing. She reached for him, guiding him to her center.

He entered her slowly, dipping the tip in first, letting her moisture surround him and ease his penetration.

Leilani didn't care about moving slowly. She wanted him inside her, moving in and out, filling the emptiness she hadn't known existed until Angel had made her so painfully and exquisitely aware.

She grasped his buttocks and pulled him closer

until he was fully sheathed inside her. Only then did she feel whole.

For years, she'd thought her life perfect, content to run her businesses and paint when she could.

Having Angel with her that day, watching over her, and now moving inside her, she realized there was more to life than her lone existence. He made her yearn for his touch, to need him like a crop needs rain.

Angel started slow, moving in and out, increasing his speed each time until he pumped faster and faster.

Leilani rose to him, meeting his thrusts, driving him deeper. Soon, he was rocking the bed with the force of his desire.

On his last thrust, he went deep, burying himself inside her, his body still, his cock pulsing his release.

For a long time, he remained suspended above her, his eyes closed, his face tight.

Then he collapsed on top of her and lay there for a moment, breathing hard, his skin shiny from exertion.

With his weight pressing her into the mattress, Leilani could barely breathe. She didn't mind...for a while.

Angel stirred and rolled onto his side, slipping free of Leilani. He ran his hand down her arm and rested it on her hip. "Are you all right?"

She drew a deep breath and let it out, a smile lifting her lips. "Better than all right."

He chuckled. "For the record, you're amazing."

"Ditto." She turned on her side to face him. "I was going to suggest we go for a walk down by the beach and maybe go swimming, sans suits."

"Did you change your mind?" he asked.

"No. In fact, I'm even more intrigued." She nestled closer to him, resting her head in the crook of his shoulder. "I've been fantasizing about swimming naked with you since our little bit of snorkeling this afternoon. I've lived around the ocean all my life and have never made love in the water."

"That would be a first for me as well." He patted her hip. "I'm in. Although, if you want to make love on the beach, it's a hard pass for me."

"Me, too." Leilani trailed her finger across his chest. "There's nothing sexy about getting sand in places that sand should never be."

He captured her finger and carried it to his lips. "Now you've done it."

Leilani frowned. "Done what?"

"Got me fixated on the image of you and me making love in the ocean." He slapped her ass playfully and leaned up on his elbow. "Come on, woman. Let's go."

"What?" She lay on the bed, staring up at him. "I'm still basking in the afterglow of deliciously hot sex.

I'm pretty certain my legs are boneless and won't carry me to the door, much less all the way out to the water."

"You won't know until you try." Angel kissed her, rolled out of the bed and stood, all muscles and male gorgeousness.

Leilani's pulse quickened. "You're inspiring me."

"Good. We might want to wear suits on our way there."

She nodded. "We wouldn't want to shock anyone who might be out for a stroll in the starlight."

"Yeah. But all bets and clothes off when we reach the water."

"I think I've created a monster," Leilani groused, though he didn't have to twist her arm to motivate her. His naked body was enough to reignite the flame of her desire. She was already aroused again without even touching him.

Leilani scooted off the bed and headed for the bathroom. She made sure to swing her hips with a little more oomph as she passed Angel, hoping to fire up his engine as much as he had hers.

She'd just made it past him when he reached out, hooked his arm around her waist and pulled her back against his front.

His still-hard cock nudged the crease between her butt cheeks. "Keep that up, and we won't make it to the water. We might not even make it out of this room."

Leilani leaned back, grinding her bottom against his shaft. "I can wait until we get to the water. Can you?"

His hands slipped around to her front, his fingers diving between her folds to stroke her clit. "Are you sure about that?" His finger touched her sweet spot, sending bursts of sensation shooting through her.

Leilani's breath caught. "Touché," she said, her voice breathy.

He released her and stepped away. "Two minutes."

"I can be ready in one," she said, her voice husky with desire. Leilani dove into the bathroom, grabbed her bikini from where she'd hung it on the shower rod to dry and quickly pulled it on.

She slid her feet into a pair of flip-flops, grabbed a towel and hurried out into the living area. "Ready?"

Angel stood by the door, wearing his swim trunks and flip-flops. He held up the key to the door and a condom packet. "Ready."

He pulled the door open and stepped out first, looking all around.

Leilani waited inside until he waved her through.

She pulled the door shut behind them, hooked her hand through the crook of Angel's elbow and led him down the path to the beach.

Lights shone around the edges of the curtains of the other suites, but no one came out.

It wasn't all that late, but the families were in for

the night, probably herding their children through baths to get to bed before nine o'clock.

Once they passed the last building, Leilani and Angel had the path to themselves. Bright starlight lit the sky, making it easy to find their way down to the water.

Leilani looked from one end of the stretch of beach to the other. Nothing moved, and she didn't see any shadowy figures lying in the sand. They had the beach all to themselves.

She reached to untie the strap tied behind her back. When she raised her hands to the bow at the base of her neck, she looked around again. Though she didn't see anyone, a creepy feeling washed over her as if someone was watching her.

Leilani retied the strap at the middle of her back.

Angel stood with his hands on the waistband of his swim trunks, a frown denting his brow. "I never turn down an opportunity to skinny dip," he said. "But I have a funny feeling about this."

"You, too?" Leilani asked, her gaze also sweeping the beach for any sign of trouble. "Would it help to walk it to see if we're missing something or someone?"

"Yeah, let's do that." He held out his arm, and Leilani hooked her elbow around his. Then, they set off at a brisk pace, walking along the shore.

Besides the occasional clump of lava rock and a couple of palms, the beach was empty.

Leilani turned toward the stand of palms they'd passed through on the path down from the buildings. The area beneath them was completely cloaked in shadows. Short of searching through the small forest, they had no way of knowing if someone was there, watching them.

With a sigh, Leilani turned to Angel, her lips twisting into a grimace.

"Not feeling it, are you?" he said.

She shook her head. "I can't shake the feeling we're being watched."

"Same." He stared at the shadows beneath the palms. "Although I don't give a rat's ass if anyone gets an eyeful of my fine physique, I don't want to expose you to some peeping Tom who's lurking in the dark, hoping to get an eyeful of a pretty, naked female."

"I want a raincheck for another night." Leilani wrapped her arms around Angel's middle and rested her cheek against his chest. She could hear the reassuring beat of his heart. For a long moment, she stood in his arms, not caring if someone say them holding each other in the moonlight.

Unlike Angel, Leilani had no desire to strip naked in front of a peeping Tom.

They might not swim naked that night, but Leilani vowed to do it another night when she didn't have that nagging tug of paranoia.

She lifted her head, stared up into Angel's gaze

and smiled. "At least we had a lovely walk on the beach."

"Yes, we did." He brushed a strand of her hair back behind her ear. "We should call it a night and get some rest. Are you going out with Windsong II tomorrow?"

Leilani shrugged. "I'll be there in the morning and make my decision then. I fully expect we'll lose some of our reservations. Word gets out fast around the island. We might even lose some of our deckhands since we're down one boat and might have to shut down operations until we can stop the attacks. In that case, I'll need to be there to fill in."

Back at her suite, Angel tapped the key card over the lock and pushed the door open. "Let me check."

Leilani didn't argue. She waited patiently outside the suite while Angel searched her apartment.

Thankfully, it was clear. Angel could imagine Leilani thinking his insistence on checking her room was a waste of time.

He didn't care. Better safe than dead.

Once they were safely inside, he stood in the living area, at a loss for what to do next.

Yeah, they'd made love, but he couldn't assume she wanted him to sleep with her.

Leilani disappeared into the bedroom.

A moment later, she reappeared in the doorway, a frown creasing her brow. "Aren't you coming?"

He remained standing in the other room. "Only if that's what you want."

Her frown deepened. Leilani left her bedroom, crossed to where he stood, took his hand and led him into the bedroom.

That night, they made love slowly and intentionally, fully aware of the other's needs. Angel made certain he satisfied her desires before slaking his own.

It was well past midnight when Leilani fell asleep, a smile on her face.

Angel lay for a few minutes longer, staring down at Leilani, marveling at her beauty and how freely she'd opened to him.

He found himself wondering if there was a world where he and Leilani had a future together.

His career path led to the Big Island. Leilani loved her birthright there on Maui. Angel doubted she'd willingly leave to follow any man anywhere else.

Which left him where?

Completely infatuated with a woman who would never be with him. A woman who would choose her island over him.

When this case was over, he'd move on. Leilani would stay on Maui and pick up the pieces of the only life she'd ever known. It would never be how it had been before the fires, but it was still the island of her ancestors. That was reason enough to make her want to stay.

As he held her in his arms, he couldn't imagine life without this woman. A woman he'd known less than a week.

He vowed to make the most of the rest of his week with Leilani, stockpiling memories as that might be all he had left of her once he left Maui.

CHAPTER 11

Leilani woke with a smile, her body tucked against Angel's, wishing she could always wake this way.

Though she'd rather lay there all morning, safe and warm, she had responsibilities to her employees, her business and the customers who'd reserved space on her tour boat, the Windsong II.

She'd done her best to accommodate the guests who'd been assigned to the now-defunct Windsong I by shifting many over to crowd onto the Windsong II. Unfortunately, she wasn't able to get them all onto the other boat. She'd managed to work with other tour companies to reassign them to similar tours, canceling their reservations with Windsong Tours and transferring them to her competitors.

It was what they did. Her competitors were her peers, not her enemies. They helped each other out when a boat had to go into the shop unexpectedly.

They did their best to keep the customers happy no matter what tour company benefitted. They counted on each other to help out when they needed it.

Leilani slipped out of bed, careful not to wake Angel. She grabbed a T-shirt from a drawer, entered the bathroom and closed the door to avoid disturbing him. After brushing her teeth and pulling her hair back into a ponytail, she left the bathroom to find the bed empty.

"Angel?" she called out.

"In here," he answered from the living area.

She found him fully dressed in swim trunks and a polo shirt, sitting on the sofa, tying the strings on his running shoes.

"What do you usually do for breakfast," he asked.

"Give me a minute to get the rest of my clothes on, and I'll make scrambled eggs." She stripped out of the T-shirt, pulled on a bikini and topped it with a Windsong polo shirt and shorts. She shoved her feet into deck shoes and hurried out to the living area, anxious to be with Angel. She found that the more she was with him, the more she wanted to be with him.

She didn't want to think about the end of the week when he'd leave for the Big Island and his new job with the Brotherhood Protectors.

Angel stood at the two-burner stove in the tiny kitchenette. His height and broad shoulders filled the space, making it impossible for two people to be there at once. In the short time it had taken her to dress, he'd found a pan, cooking spray and eggs and was well into cooking scrambled eggs.

Even though there wasn't really enough room in the kitchen for anyone else, Leilani squeezed past Angel and pulled plates and a toaster out of cabinets. She plugged in the toaster and slid two slices of bread into the slots.

"Coffee?" she asked.

"Absolutely," he answered, busily pushing the fluffy yellow eggs around the skillet.

Leilani spooned coffee grounds into a fresh filter and poured water into the coffeemaker. Minutes later, the rich scent filled the kitchen.

When the toast popped up, Leilani buttered one side and laid a slice on each plate.

Angel scooped scrambled eggs from the pan onto the two plates and set the pan to soak in the sink.

Leilani carried the plates to the small table and went back to the coffee maker to fill two cups with the steaming brew.

Angel took one from her, then bent and brushed his lips across hers. "Good morning, beautiful."

Her entire body warmed at his kiss and words. They dispelled any awkward, morning-after anxiety she'd felt.

They carried their mugs to the table and dug into the food.

Halfway through the eggs on her plate, Leilani's

cell phone chirped with an incoming text. She glanced down at a message from Captain Dave.

Steve called in sick. Brad showed up coughing. Sent him home. Tried to get Josh. Not answering. Need deckhands ASAP.

Leilani sighed. "Captain Dave just informed me his deckhands are out sick. If I can't get anyone else to come in on short notice, I'll be working on the Windsong II today."

"Don't forget, Reid will be there to take over from Dev."

Leilani called Josh's number. His voicemail picked up immediately, so she left a message. "Hey, Josh, this is Leilani. Captain Dave's deckhands are out sick. Need you to work the Windsong II today. Call me when you get this message."

After she ended the call, she quickly finished her breakfast and carried her plate and Angel's to the little sink, rinsed them and tucked them into the miniature dishwasher.

"I just need to brush my teeth, and I'll be ready to go. Do I need to get my car keys from Olina?"

Angel carried their coffee mugs to the sink. "No. We'll take the rental for as long as I'm here." While Leilani rinsed the mugs and stacked them in the dishwasher, Angel grabbed his shaving kit.

They converged in the bathroom to brush their teeth, sharing the sink like a married couple.

Leilani liked that it felt natural, free of any kind of

embarrassment. Damn, she could get used to having him around on a more permanent basis.

She sighed and spit toothpaste into the sink.

Angel did as well and met her gaze in the mirror. "That was a big sigh. Did I keep you up too late, and now you're too tired to work the tour?"

"No, I'm fine," she said, her cheeks heating. "Just thinking about all the things I need to do."

Angel rinsed his toothbrush, then tapped the excess water out.

Leilani hung her toothbrush in the holder. "You can put yours here with mine if you like."

He did. The simple gesture was one more way of reminding Leilani what life would be like if they could be together every day.

She pushed thoughts of a future without Angel out of her mind, squared her shoulders and prepared to face the day.

Halfway across the resort campus, Angel's cell phone chirped. He fished it out of his pocket and looked at the screen. "It's Swede, Hank's computer guy." He answered the call. "Cortez, here."

Leilani leaned close in an attempt to hear what Swede had to say.

"Hang on," Angel said. "Let me put you on speaker so Leilani can hear as well." He switched the phone to speaker.

"Good morning, Leilani," Swede said. "I wanted to

bring you up to date on what I've found on the names of the people Cortez gave me to dig into."

"Anything interesting?" Angel asked.

"Maybe," Swede said. "You've met these people. I'll let you decide. First, I searched the internet for information on the broker, Peter Brentwood. He's a high-dollar broker out of California who helps large corporations find properties that meet their investment and or expansion needs. He's racked up a lot of money in commissions and has been a top earner for the past five years. Some of the most noteworthy properties he brokered had articles identifying him as the man who'd cut the deal. He's had a couple of lawsuits filed against him, accusing him of using strong-arm tactics to get the owners to sell. The cases were dropped due to lack of substantial evidence."

Leilani's gaze met Angel's. "He's been very persistent, but we haven't caught him in the act."

"That could be his MO," Swede said.

"Anything else on him?" Angel asked.

"As much money as he's made, he doesn't have a lot to show for it. When his second wife divorced him recently, she took him to the cleaners. She got the house in California, the one in Florida and most of the money in his bank accounts. He got the credit card debt and the attorney's fees for both sides."

"He needs to refill his bank accounts," Angel said.

Leilani nodded. "Being broke is a strong incentive

to land a big deal. Did you find out who he's representing in his campaign to buy my property?"

"Starlight Resorts International," Swede said. "They have resorts all over the world, except in Hawaii. They prefer to build from the ground up rather than purchasing existing properties. When they go after a particular property, they give huge incentives to the people who help them close the deal."

"All the more reason for Brentwood to use whatever methods at his disposal to make it happen." Angel's brow creased heavily. "We'll keep an eye on him."

"What else?" Leilani prompted.

"I searched for information on Buddy Akina," Swede said. "He's been arrested several times for trespassing on private property. There was a big article about him claiming the properties belonged to the native Hawaiians. They were sacred to his people and should never have been sold. He has organized sit-ins blocking construction workers from building or expanding resorts. He was sued for destruction of property when he pulled a fence down and blocked access to a beach. Charges were dropped, and the fence remained down."

Leilani's lips curled. "I can't picture Buddy driving a jet boat and crashing it into a boat full of people. He wants to limit tourism on Maui, but not by killing or injuring anyone."

"I did a search on Leilani's cousin, Makai Kealoha."

Leilani's gaze shot to Angel.

"I had him look at anyone who might have a reason to want to hurt your business," Angel said. "He might harbor resentment that you inherited family property, and he didn't."

"Most of what I found on Makai had to do with his surfing competitions. He's done well for himself. If not winning, he's at least placed second and third in a number of competitions."

"Second and third are amazing, but don't get the big cash prizes," Leilani murmured.

"He's listed as one of the Lahaina residents whose home burned to the ground," Swede continued.

Leilani nodded. "He had just sunk a bunch of money into remodeling before his wedding."

"That would explain why he's got significant credit card debt," Swede said.

Leilani frowned. "You can see that kind of information?"

Swede didn't answer but continued with, "Quite a few articles about Makai linked him to another surfer, Alyssa Matson."

"His fiancée," Leilani said.

"Right," Swede concurred. "Each of the articles made a point of showcasing their romance. One article went so far as to dub them the sweetheart couple of the surfing scene."

"Makai is crazy about her," Leilani said. "They both love surfing above all else. Makai works at the resort not because he loves his job and wants to make it a career but because he wants to fund his real passion."

"Surfing," Angel concluded.

"While I was looking into Makai, I ran a search for information about Alyssa." Swede paused.

Leilani's eyes narrowed. "Find anything?"

"Not much more than what I found on Makai. I did find an arrest record from several years back when she was nineteen years old."

"Arrested for what?" This was the first she'd heard about problems with her future cousin-in-law.

"Assault and battery," Swede said. "The victim was a female surfer. Apparently, the woman had placed first in a competition and made it a point to rub it in Alyssa's face. Alyssa beat the shit out of her. Local law enforcement covering the competition had to pull Alyssa off the woman."

"Seriously?" Leilani shook her head. "Did she serve time?"

"No," Swede said. "The judge sentenced her to probation and six months of anger management therapy. She also has several credit cards, all maxed out to the tune of thirty thousand dollars."

Leilani whistled. "I wonder if Makai knows what he's getting into?"

Angel's brows lowered as his gaze locked with

Leilani's. "Has she displayed any violent tendencies around you?"

"Not in front of me." Leilani thought back to the times she'd been with Makai and Alyssa. His fiancée had always been close to him, touching his arm, giving him an occasional kiss. "I've never even seen her raise her voice. And the credit card debt could be from what she's been spending on her wedding."

Leilani hated the idea of Makai and Alyssa starting their marriage so deeply in debt.

"That's all I've found so far," Swede said. "I'll keep you informed of anything else that crops up."

"Thanks," Angel said.

After the call ended, Leilani glanced at the clock on her cell phone. "Shoot. We need to get moving. We'll need to help get the boat ready."

"Reid's probably already there to relieve Dev."

"Yeah, but he won't know everything the deckhands have to prepare," Leilani said.

Angel held her door for her as she slipped into the passenger seat of his rental car. Once she was buckled in, he closed her door and hurried to slide in behind the steering wheel.

He drove a few miles per hour over the speed limit to get them there as quickly as possible. They had to stop at the grocery store close to the harbor to purchase several bags of ice and pick up the food and drinks she'd preordered for pickup that morning.

By the time they pulled into the marina parking

lot, they were twenty minutes later than Leilani had wanted to arrive.

He'd barely shifted into park when Leilani hopped out of the car. "I'll get the cart to haul all of this to the boat.

She hurried to the shed between the parking lot and the jetty.

Rather than stay with the car, Angel followed.

He hadn't been kidding when he'd told her he would stay with her twenty-four-seven. She smiled to herself as she unlocked the shed and pulled out the utility cart they used to move supplies.

Angel took over and wheeled the cart back to the parking lot. Together, they loaded the food, sodas and ice onto the cart.

Once they had everything, Angel pushed the cart out onto the dock, bumping across the wooden planks to where the Windsong II was moored.

Captain Dave waved at them from his perch at the helm on the upper deck. "Got a call from Josh; he's on his way. He'll be here just in time to go out with us."

Reid straightened from sorting through the life vests. "You just missed Dev. He said he'd work the tour, but I sent him back to the resort. He needed a shower and a real bed."

"Did he say how it went last night?" Angel asked.

"Good until two charter boats came in after dark. They tied off in a couple of the slips. The people on board stayed, playing loud music and drinking until well after midnight." Reid shook his head. "Dev didn't get much sleep."

While Angel and Reid helped Leilani unload the cart onto the boat, Makai appeared on the dock.

Leilani joined him, her brow furrowing. "Hey cousin, what brings you to the harbor so early?"

"Late last night, I heard someone ran into one of your tour boats yesterday. I wanted to call you then, but it was already pretty late, and I didn't want to wake you." He gripped her shoulders and stared down at her. "Are you all right?"

She nodded. "I am."

"Anyone hurt badly?" he asked.

Leilani shook her head. "Nothing more than a few bumps and scrapes. The boat took the worst of it. It's in the shop. Hopefully, they'll fix it right up. My crew can't work without a boat. And now, the crew for this boat called in sick. That's why we're late getting started."

Makai clapped his hands together. "What can I do to help? I have the day off. I can go with the boat and hand out life vests and drinks."

Leilani leaned up on her toes and brushed a kiss across his cheek. "Thank you for caring. If you really want to help, you can take the cart to the shed, grab the two big ice chests and bring them down to the dock for me." She handed him the key to the lock on the shed. "Josh is on his way here. Between Josh, Reid and me, I think we can take care of every challenge that arises."

"I would love to help out," Makai said. "I'm on the water every day, all day, but on a board. It would be nice to experience the water from a boat I don't have to drive. And it's been a long time since I've been snorkeling. I could help your guests see the amazing sea life here on Maui. But I wouldn't want to be in the way."

Leilani smiled. "I thought you spent every day surfing."

Makai grinned. "Not every day."

"From what Alyssa told me, you have a major competition coming up soon. How does she feel about having you play hooky from training?"

"Shh," he said, raising his finger to his lips. "She doesn't know I'm here. She thinks I'm surfing."

Leilani shook her head. "If she asks me where you are, I'm not lying for you."

Makai nodded, a smile tilting the corners of his lips. "Deal. Now, where are those ice chests?" He glanced around. "Oh, yes, you said something about a shed."

"The shed is where we store supplies, scuba tanks, apparatus, wetsuits, and toiletries. It's also where we store our ice chests." She pointed to a row of sheds between the docks and the parking lot. "It's the second one from the left. I'm going to toss stuff in the refrigerator and then join you at the shed to see if there's anything else we might need to take with us today." She handed the key to Makai.

He turned and headed for the shed.

Leilani moved the sandwiches to the refrigerator.

Angel laid the bags of ice in the bar sink.

"I'm going up to the shed," she said, leaving the boat.

Like a shadow she couldn't shake, Angel fell in step with her. She reached for his hand.

He took it and held it firmly.

Ahead, Makai had reached the shed. When he raised his hand with the key to unload the door, he paused, frowning. "Hey, Leilani, was the shed supposed to be locked?"

Leilani shook her head. "Yes. Why?"

"It's not locked now." Makai stood to the side so Leilani could see for herself. "In fact, there's no padlock."

Angel stepped between Leilani and the shed. "Stay back and let me look."

Leilani gripped Makai's arm and pulled him back a few steps.

Angel pushed the door inward and peered inside.

Leilani stepped up beside him. "What? No boogieman?"

"Nobody hiding inside," he announced. "Looks like a shed full of supplies, scuba and spearfishing gear."

"That's what it is," she said, moving forward with

every intention of grabbing one of the heavy ice chests.

Angel gripped her arm, bringing her to a halt. "We'll load them." He pushed past her and grabbed one of the big chests. As he stepped out of the shed, Makai entered and grabbed the other chest.

When he dragged the chest toward him, one of the spearfishing guns tipped over. As it teetered, Leilani noticed it had a spear loaded in it. They never stored them loaded.

"Wait!" she called out a second too late.

The gun fell, bounced against a box and discharged.

Makai dropped the ice chest to the ground and slumped over it, cursing, "Fuck. Fuck. Fuck. What the hell?"

"Oh, sweet Jesus." With her heart in her throat, Leilani rushed forward and wrapped her arm around her cousin to keep him from falling. When she saw what had happened, her stomach clenched.

The spear had pierced Makai's thigh, the arrow-head embedded in the thickest part of his muscle.

Makai's dark skin blanched white, and his eyes rolled backward.

Leilani cried out, "Angel. Help me."

CHAPTER 12

ANGEL HAD TURNED AWAY, carrying the big ice chest, when he heard the speargun discharge. When he glanced over his shoulder to see what had happened, he heard Leilani's cry for help.

He dropped the ice chest and leaped toward Leilani and Makai, catching them both before Makai's weight took them to the ground.

Angel and Leilani struggled to hold him upright long enough for Angel to assess the position of the spear. Then they eased him to the ground on his side, careful not to bump the spear and send it deeper into his leg.

As soon as they safely got Leilani's cousin on the ground, his eyes blinked open, and he started to sit up.

Angel held him down. "Don't move." To Leilani, he said, "Call 911."

She was already halfway there, having pulled her cell phone out of her pocket and hitting the emergency feature.

"What happened?" Makai asked.

"A spearfishing gun went off, and you're the unlucky recipient of a spear in your leg," Angel informed him.

Makai leaned his head up and frowned at the spear jutting from his thigh. "Get it out," he said roughly, reaching for the spear.

Angel grabbed his hand. "Don't touch it. The arrow's point is embedded in your leg. If you try to remove it, it will do more damage than it already has, and you could bleed out. You'll have to have it surgically removed. Leilani's on the phone with 911 to get an ambulance here. In the meantime, you need to stay still."

Makai's face was pale, his jaw tight. "It hurts like a motherfucker."

"Yeah. I can only imagine. I've been hit with shrapnel, but never a spear from a speargun."

Leilani ended the call and turned to her cousin. "An ambulance is on the way."

"Hey," Josh Wright, the deckhand from Windsong II, jogged up to them. "What's going on?" He glanced down at Makai, and his eyes widened. "Holy shit. What happened?"

Leilani's lips pressed into a tight line. "The speargun was left loaded and propped against the wall in the shed. When Makai pulled the ice chest out, it fell and discharged."

"We never store the speargun loaded," Josh said.

Leilani nodded. "Exactly. Do you know who was the last one to use it?"

"Hell, it hasn't been used since before the fire. It's been in the shed the entire time." Josh's brow knitted. "I know for a fact it wasn't loaded yesterday when we stowed the ice chests in the shed. Hell, it was hung on the rack above the spare life vests." He pointed to the empty rack. "Who would take it down, load it and leave it where it could fall and go off?"

"I'd like to know the answer to that question myself," Leilani said, her tone tight, angry. "I'll be back in a minute. I want to talk with Captain Dave." She glanced down at her cousin. "Are you hanging in there?"

Makai grimaced. "As well as to be expected with a spear sticking out of my leg." He moved slightly and winced. "All I can think is that it's better that it hit me, not you."

Leilani reached for his hand and squeezed it gently. "I'd rather it had been me. This shouldn't have happened to you. The one time you came to the dock to see me, this has to happen."

He squeezed her hand. "As short as you are, that spear would've hit you low in your groin or belly. I'll be okay."

She held on a moment longer, then bent to press a

kiss to his forehead. "I miss how close we were as kids before our grandfather passed."

Makai nodded. "Me, too. My father cashed in on his inheritance and squandered it. Your dad did it right. Did you know he offered me a job?"

Leilani nodded.

"I didn't take it because I didn't want charity or hard feelings between us. I wanted to make it on my own, surfing." He shifted slightly and winced. "Jesus."

"The ambulance will be here soon," Leilani said. "Maybe they'll give you something for the pain. I need to see Captain Dave for a minute, then I'll be back to ride with you to the hospital."

"You don't have to go with me," Makai said. "You have a tour to guide."

"Josh is here now. Between him and Reid, they can handle it." She patted his shoulder. "I'm going with you."

Leilani hurried to the dock and walked out to the boat.

Angel's gaze followed her. He didn't like that she was so far away. If something happened to her, he wouldn't be right there to protect her.

"Leilani is one of the nicest people you'll ever meet," Makai said, his words strained through clenched teeth. "Her father was the same. I came down here today because I'd heard about what happened yesterday with someone crashing into her boat. I took the day off to go with her on the water. I'm worried about her."

"Me, too." Angel's gaze stayed with Leilani as she stopped to talk to Reid.

Reid shot a glance toward Makai. He and Leilani exchanged a few words while Reid's gaze remained fixed on Angel and Makai.

Leilani left Reid and then climbed to the upper deck to speak with Captain Dave. He came to the edge of the deck and stared across the distance to where Angel waited with Makai, his brow deeply furrowed.

Angel's cell phone chirped with an incoming text. He pulled it from his pocket. It was a text from Reid.

Reid: It wasn't an accident, was it?

Angel: No

Reid: Fuck

Angel: Yeah

Leilani came down from the top deck, followed by Captain Dave. They stopped to talk to Reid and Josh. The two men nodded and went to work on the deck, gathering life vests.

Leilani hugged Captain Dave, left the boat and hurried back across the dock.

Sirens sounded nearby. By the time Leilani made it back to where her cousin lay by the shed, the ambulance had arrived.

"I'm suspending tour operations until further notice," she said.

"I'm sorry, Leilani," Makai said.

She looked at him, her brow wrinkling. "Why are you sorry? You didn't do this. You didn't ask to be skewered by a speargun. I can't in good conscience send my crew and guests out, knowing there's a chance they might be attacked like we were yesterday. I should have canceled operations yesterday. If I had, you wouldn't have been shot in the leg."

Angel frowned. "You can't blame yourself,"

"He's right," Makai said. "You didn't shoot me."

"No, but I should've shut down after the crash." She lifted her chin. "It's done now, and since it's too late to let the guests know, Captain Dave will greet them and let them know I'll refund their money. In the meantime, you're going to a hospital to get that thing out of your leg."

"I'm all for that." Makai's face was pale, and he was turning slightly gray around his lips.

The emergency medical technicians eased Makai onto a stretcher. Angel helped to stabilize the leg with the spear until they could get him onto the stretcher and into the back of the ambulance.

Makai passed out halfway through the effort.

Angel was glad for him. The pain had to be excruciating.

Once Makai was secured in the ambulance, Leilani climbed in with him.

"I'll follow," Angel said.

She gave him a tight smile. "Thank you."

The door closed between them, and the ambulance pulled away, lights flashing.

Angel ran for the rental car and quickly caught up with the ambulance. The more he thought about that spearfishing gun, the sicker it made him. If Leilani had pulled the ice chest out of the shed, that spear could have killed her.

MAKAI REMAINED unconscious during the ride to the hospital.

Leilani used the time to call his fiancée. Makai would want her there with him.

Alyssa's phone rang five times and went to her voicemail.

"Hey, Alyssa, this is Leilani. There's been an accident. They're transporting Makai to the hospital. Please meet me there." She'd thought about explaining more about the injury but figured it would be too much for a voicemail. Hearing it in person would be better. Hopefully, the doctor would have a chance to evaluate and determine a course of action by the time Alyssa arrived.

Leilani looked at the spear jutting out of her cousin's leg, her stomach roiling. Makai was her only living relative. If that spear had gone in any other direction, it could have killed him. Memories of their childhood played through her mind like silent movies. They'd played together at family gatherings, back when their grandparents had still been alive, with their parents nearby, swapping stories about their childhoods. They'd been happy and carefree, with a bright future and love all around.

Upon arriving at the hospital, the medics helped Leilani out of the back of the ambulance and then eased the stretcher out, dropping the wheels to the ground.

Leilani followed Makai into the emergency department. After a quick evaluation by the ER doctor on duty, he was wheeled into an operating room where a surgeon was already preparing for the surgery.

A nurse directed Leilani to a waiting room.

When Angel entered the room, Leilani walked straight into his open arms.

For a long moment, she stood there, absorbing his strength.

"I'm ready for this nightmare to be over," she murmured against his chest.

"I know." He stroked the back of her hair. "Me, too. I keep thinking that could've been you."

"Or Josh or Captain Dave," she added. "But it wasn't. It was my cousin. He wasn't even supposed to be there. If they're trying to target my business, why can't they limit their aim to me?"

He pulled her closer. "No one should be targeting anyone. This has to stop."

"Agreed," she said and looked up into Angel's eyes.

"But how can we stop someone when we don't know who it is?"

Angel opened his mouth to respond, but a voice cut him off.

"Holy shit, Leilani, what the hell happened?"

ANGEL AND LEILANI turned to find Alyssa standing in the doorway to the waiting room. She wore a swimsuit coverup belted at the waist, damp from what appeared to be a bikini beneath it, and flip-flops on her feet.

Leilani stepped out of Angel's arms and met Alyssa halfway across the room. "What do you know so far?"

"Just what you left on my voicemail. The receptionist at the desk directed me to the surgical waiting room."

Angel moved to stand beside Leilani.

She drew in a deep breath and let it out slowly. "He was shot by a speargun."

"Wait..." Alyssa shook her head, her brow wrinkling. "What?"

"He was helping me get the boat ready for a tour. When he pulled the ice chest out of the shed, a speargun fell and discharged a spear. It lodged in his leg."

"Are you serious?" Alyssa pushed her damp hair back from her forehead. "Why was he helping you get a tour ready? We were supposed to be surfing together this morning. He told me he had to work. And who the hell stores a loaded speargun? That's pure homicidal negligence. What kind of business are you running? No wonder it's falling apart. You should've let those damned boats burn with everything else. That spear could've killed Makai—all because of your incompetence at running your business."

Leilani's head snapped back as if she'd been struck.

Angel stepped between the two women, anger pushing adrenaline through his system. He didn't want to make matters worse for Leilani, but he wouldn't stand by and let Alyssa blame her for what had happened. "Leilani was as much a victim as Makai. She did not store a loaded speargun, and neither did her employees. Someone tampered with it and positioned it where it would fall and trigger the release. Makai was the unlucky one to be on the receiving end."

Alyssa glared up into Angel's eyes, red-faced and nostrils flaring. "Makai never should have been there in the first place. He has a ridiculous sense of responsibility toward Leilani, even though *she* inherited everything, and he got nothing. And yet, she expects him to bail her out when shit happens." She stepped to the side of Angel and jabbed her finger at Leilani. "I call bullshit. You're nothing but a drain on Makai.

If not for you, he'd have left Maui a long time ago. We could've lived on Oahu, had jobs that paid better and been closer to the real waves and surfing community."

Leilani's face blanched. "He thinks I'm a drain on him?"

"Of course you are. He knows you're not capable of running your father's business. You should've sold it when your father died. You should sell it now."

Leilani's eyes filled with tears.

Her tears pierced Angel's heart as sharply as the spear had cleaved her cousin's leg. His hands clenched into fists. Again, he stepped in front of Alyssa. "Stop."

"No. She needs to hear this. I've kept my mouth shut for too long. She doesn't care about Makai or the people who work for her. She only cares about herself and what money she can make at others' expense."

Rage burned in Angel's chest. He had to fight for control. Had Alyssa been a man spewing that kind of hatred and lies, Angel would have punched him in the face. The urge to punch Alyssa was so strong he had to focus on dragging in steady breaths to keep from losing his shit. He'd never hit a woman. But, damn, he wanted to hit this one.

When a hand touched his arm, Angel flinched.

"It's okay," Leilani said. "She's upset."

"She's wrong," he said through gritted teeth. "I've

seen how you are with your employees. You care about them. They're as much a part of your life as family."

Alyssa snorted. "Which isn't saying much since she brought this on her only relative. This is all your fault. You shouldn't even be here."

Leilani stepped up beside Angel, her chin up. "However you feel about me right now isn't important. What's important is Makai. You might hate me, but I'm not going anywhere until I know my cousin is okay." Leilani spun on her heel, walked to the farthest corner of the waiting room and dropped into a seat.

Alyssa glared at her the whole way. When she opened her mouth, Angel held up his hand. "You've said more than enough." He didn't wait for a response. Instead, he crossed the room and sat beside Leilani, wrapped his arm around her and held her.

She looked calm and unaffected, but her body trembled beneath his arm.

Angel wanted to pull her closer, but he suspected she was holding it together by a thread and didn't want to disturb her concentration.

For the next hour, Alyssa paced. Leilani sat silently, staring at the door. Angel stayed at her side. He couldn't undo what Alyssa had said or take away the pain it had caused Leilani, but he could be there for her.

Then, a man dressed in surgical scrubs entered

the waiting room and looked around. "Family of Mr. Kealoha?"

Alyssa hurried forward. "I'm his fiancée."

Leilani rose and walked toward the doctor. "I'm Leilani Kealoha, his cousin and only living relative."

Alyssa's gaze shot daggers at Leilani.

Angel took up a position between Alyssa and Leilani. "I'm here with Ms. Kealoha."

The doctor's gaze went from Alyssa to Leilani and settled on Angel. "I'm Dr. Dutton. I performed the procedure on Mr. Kealoha. The spear pierced Mr. Kealoha's right thigh. Fortunately, it missed his femoral artery, or he would've bled out before they got him to the hospital. He'll need time for the muscle to heal and physical therapy. He's doing well and in recovery."

Leilani slipped her arm around Angel's back and leaned into him. "Thank God."

"So, he'll have a full recovery?" Alyssa asked.

The doctor nodded. "He should."

"Good," she said with a smile. "He's been accepted into the Eddie surfing competition."

The doctor's brow dipped. "Isn't that next month?"

Alyssa nodded. "I had to pull a lot of strings to get invited. It'll be our first time at the Eddie, and we're doing it together."

The doctor was shaking his head before Alyssa finished. "You don't understand. He'll have to stay off that leg for several weeks to give the muscle a chance to heal. Then, he'll only be able to bear a little weight for a while and have to go through months of physical therapy to rebuild the damaged muscle. You're looking at five or six months at the earliest before he can surf again."

Alyssa's eyes narrowed. "You're kidding me, right? He's supposed to surf the Eddie next month. He has to. So much is riding on his being there."

The doctor met Alyssa's gaze and held it. "Mr. Kealoha will not be surfing in anything next month. He'll barely be able to stand. If he wants to regain full use of that leg, he's got to give it time to heal." The doctor stepped back. "He'll be here a couple of days. When he's released, he'll be moved to a rehabilitation facility. The wound will need care until it closes. I'll be by to check in on him before I leave this afternoon. You'll be allowed into the recovery room for a few minutes once he regains consciousness. When he's stable, he'll be moved to a room."

"Thank you, Dr. Dutton," Leilani said.

The doctor turned to leave, then paused and looked back at Alyssa. "If the spear had been a fraction of an inch over, it would've severed the femoral artery. Your fiancé is lucky to be alive."

The doctor left the waiting room.

Alyssa remained standing where he'd left her, her face drained of color.

Leilani took a step toward Alyssa.

Angel touched her arm and shook his head.

A nurse entered the room. "Mr. Kealoha's family?"

Leilani nodded.

"He just woke up. He's groggy and might not be awake long, but you can see him for a few minutes."

Leilani hurried after the nurse, slowing as she passed Alyssa.

Alyssa didn't move as if frozen to the floor.

Angel cupped Leilani's elbow, gently propelling her forward.

When they reached the recovery room, Leilani stood beside Makai's bed, tears filling her eyes.

Makai looked up at her. "Lani?"

"Yeah, Mak, it's me." She smiled and took his hand. "The doctor says you're going to be okay."

"He got it out?"

She nodded. "He did."

Makai closed his eyes. "Good. Didn't much like being a pin cushion."

"He said it'll take time to recover," Leilani said.

"I figured as much." Makai's voice trailed off.

Angel thought he'd fallen asleep.

Makai opened his eyes again, his mouth twisting. "Friend of mine got stabbed in the thigh when he was nightclubbing in Honolulu. Couldn't surf for months."

"You won't get to surf the Eddie," she said.

"Good," he said. "Wasn't looking forward to it, anyway. Was afraid I'd get all banged up and miss my wedding." He laughed. "Now I have no excuse. But I'll have to be in a wheelchair. Alyssa won't want to move the date again."

Leilani met Angel's gaze.

A nurse appeared.

Leilani nodded silently. "We have to go now, but I'll be back tomorrow." Leilani leaned over and pressed a kiss to Makai's forehead. "I love you, Mak."

"Love you, too, Lani." He stared across at Angel. "Take care of her."

Angel nodded. "I will."

As Leilani and Angel left the room, they found Alyssa standing in the hallway. She didn't say anything or acknowledge them as they passed by.

Angel was glad. The woman had said enough to permanently damage any relationship she might have had with Leilani.

Leilani walked out of the hospital without saying a single word.

Angel guided her across the parking lot to where he'd parked the rental car. When he opened the passenger door, Leilani practically melted into the seat.

Angel frowned. "Are you okay?"

She leaned her head back against the seat. "No."

"What can I do to help?"

She gave him a small, wry smile. "Get in the car and drive."

His lips twitched. Angel closed her door and

rounded the front of the car to slide in behind the wheel. "Back to the resort."

She shook her head. "Anywhere but there. I'm so tired of being a refugee. Tired of trying to rebuild my life. Tired of waiting to get back into Lahaina. Tired of working hard just to keep afloat." She looked out the side window. "Maybe Alyssa is right. Maybe I should sell the land in Lahaina, then take the money and go where I can paint all day and not be responsible for anyone but myself. I was a fool to think I could step into my father's shoes."

"Stop." Angel reached across the console and took her hand in his. "You're letting Alyssa get to you. She's wrong. You're good at what you do. Your people love you, and you love them. What's happened lately hasn't been because you're a bad boss. So, stop beating yourself up."

She sat for a moment, still staring out the window. "I still don't want to go back to the resort yet."

"Okay." He backed out of the parking space and shifted into the drive. "Where do you want to go?"

Leilani faced forward, her jaw set, her eyes narrowed. "Take me around Maui. Remind me why I love living here and why I shouldn't give up and leave."

Angel spent the rest of the day driving all around Maui.

Leilani showed him where to find the best hiking

trails, the most secluded waterfalls and beaches where green sea turtles came to bask in the sun.

They ate lunch at a seaside café and watched the waves wash up on shore. As the sun sank toward the horizon, Angel stopped at a beach on the west side of Maui.

They sat on the sand and watched as the clouds turned from mauve and purple to flaming orange and yellow as the sun dissolved into the ocean.

Leilani turned to Angel, cupped his cheeks in her hands and kissed him. "Thank you."

"Do you still love Maui?"

"More than ever," she responded.

"Seeing it through your eyes, I understand why. It's beautiful, amazing and magical." He brushed a strand of her dark hair back behind her ear. "I'm falling in love."

"With my island?" she whispered, her gaze seeking his.

He kissed the tip of her nose. "Yes."

"Oh."

Angel's lips curved upward. "I never believed a person could fall in love at first sight."

Her gaze shifted from his eyes to his lips. "No?"

He chuckled. "No. But I'm beginning to believe love could fall into your lap when you least expect it."

Leilani's gaze shot back up to meet his. "Are you falling in love with me?" She drew in a breath and let it out. "I hope so because I'm halfway there myself."

He pulled her closer. "Only halfway?"

She pressed her lips to his. "Mmm. Make that three-quarters of the way."

"What will it take to bring you around to one hundred percent?" Angel brushed his lips across her.

"More of this." Leilani kissed him, thrusting her tongue past his teeth.

Desire flared, sending heat throughout his body and south to his groin.

They kissed until they were forced to come up for air.

Leilani leaned her forehead against his. "I want to make love with you."

His cock twitched at her words, growing harder by the second. "Not nearly as much as I want to make love with you."

She sighed. "I'm ready to go back to the resort."

"You don't want to stay here and make love in the starlight?" he asked.

"Tempting," she said. "But remember what I said about getting sand in places sand shouldn't be?"

"Oh, yes." He grimaced. "Good point. And I'm almost sure I didn't restock my wallet with protection." He pushed to his feet and held out his hand. "Let's go."

Angel held her hand on the drive back to the resort, eager to get her alone and naked. Then he'd make love with her. By the time they were done, he hoped to have her at one hundred percent.

Though he'd never believed a person could fall in love in less than a week, he was already there—one hundred percent.

When they pulled into the parking lot, Angel shifted into park and flung open his door. He couldn't get Leilani to her room fast enough.

She was already out of the car by the time he got around to her. He took her hand in his and started walking toward her building. Their steps got faster the closer they got until they were running, laughing and ready to get behind closed doors.

Angel slowed as they rounded a corner and Leilani's building came into sight.

"Shh," Leilani pressed a finger to her lips. "We don't want anyone to know we're back. I swear Olina's kids have radar ears."

They hadn't reached her door when Angel's cell phone rang. He fumbled in his pocket in an attempt to silence the ringer before it went off again. When he pulled it out, he read the caller ID and wished he hadn't.

He frowned down at Leilani. "Sorry. I need to get this." Angel answered, "Hey, Teller, whatcha got?"

"Reid and I are on our way over to Leilani's," Teller said. "Hank and Hawk want an update on what happened today and what we want to do about it."

"It can't wait until morning?" Angel asked, knowing it couldn't. But he could always hope.

"Afraid not. Swede was able to tap into some

video surveillance systems near the harbor. He's reviewing footage as we speak and hopes to have something soon."

Angel sighed. "All right. We'll be here." He ended the call and met Leilani's gaze in the light from the corner of the building. "We're about to have company."

Leilani frowned. "I guessed as much. Hopefully, we can make it quick."

"I don't know how quick it'll be. Hank Patterson and my boss, Jace Hawkins, want to be brought up to date on what happened this morning, which shouldn't take long. But they also want to talk about what's next. I hope they have some ideas."

Leilani turned toward her building. "Let's get inside. I want to run a brush through my hair before they get here."

As Angel neared her door, something didn't feel right. The hairs on the back of his neck stood at attention.

Three steps from her door, Angel gripped Leilani's arm and pulled her back behind him.

She tensed. "What's wrong?"

"The door is open," he said softly.

"That can't be." Leilani leaned to one side, trying to look around him. "I closed it when I left."

"Shh." Angel half-turned toward her and whispered, "Go to your friend's room. Stay there until I come to get you."

Leilani shook her head. "I'm not leaving you. What if someone's inside? What if you get hurt?"

"Please. Just go," he said through clenched teeth. "I need to know you're safe."

She stared at him, her brow creased. "I don't want to scare Olina's family. If it makes you feel better, I'll hide behind the bushes."

He'd prefer she was somewhere inside a building with a door and walls between her and the bastard who'd been terrorizing her. But he understood her hesitancy to wake her friend and her children. "Fine. But stay low to the ground. We don't know if he's armed."

Leilani ducked into the bushes several yards away from her door.

When Angel was confident Leilani couldn't be seen, he eased toward the half-opened door and pushed it gently, widening the gap.

He slipped into the shadows of the sitting room, careful not to bump into the furniture.

For a long moment, he stood completely still, listening for sounds of movement. Silence reigned. Nothing moved in the living area. There was no place to hide there. Angel eased toward the bedroom door.

Was that a sound he heard? Again, he stood still and listened. Nothing.

Angel slipped through the door.

A big blob flew toward his face. He ducked and dove into the room as a pillow slammed into the door frame. By the time he rolled and sprang to his feet, the shadowy figure in black, wearing a black ski mask, raced out of the bedroom.

Angel ran after him.

By the time he reached the living area, the man was through the door and outside, darting to the left.

Angel flew out of the suite. The man ran around the corner of the next building, disappearing out of sight.

Angel followed. When he came around the same corner, he spied the man running ahead. He looked over his shoulder at Angel.

At that moment, Reid and Teller appeared ahead of the runner.

"Stop him!" Angel shouted.

The runner veered off the path, leaped over a bush, and making a wide circle, headed back the way he'd come.

When Angel tried to cut him off, he darted through some trees and headed straight for the stand of bushes close to Leilani's building.

Angel ran faster, gaining on the man.

Suddenly, the man pitched forward and face-planted on the path.

Before he could scramble to his feet, Angel landed on top of him, pinning him to the ground. The man bucked beneath him but couldn't dislodge Angel from his back.

Knowing Reid and Teller weren't far behind, Angel stayed where he was until backup reached him.

Moments later, the two men skidded to a stop beside him.

"Whatcha got there, Angel," Reid asked.

"Found him in Leilani's bedroom," Angel grunted as the man beneath him bucked.

A movement in the bushes captured Angel's attention. "Leilani?"

Branches parted, and Leilani emerged. "I stayed low," she said. "But when he ran back this way, I couldn't do nothing."

Angel sat up, grabbed the man's hand and yanked his arm up between his shoulder blades. "That was you?"

"She fucking tripped me," the man said, his face in the dirt.

Leilani shrugged. "It worked."

Angel sighed. "You could've been hurt."

"But I wasn't," she said. "Is it who I think it is?"

"Let's find out." Angel yanked the ski mask off the man's head. "Surprise. It's Peter Brentwood. Reid, please tell me you're calling 911."

CHAPTER 13

"It's ringing," Reid said and turned away. "I'd like to report an instance of breaking and entering."

Angel's cell phone rang in his back pocket. "Leilani, could you get that? My hands are full."

She plucked the phone out of his pocket, read the caller ID, answered and immediately hit the speaker button. "Hi Hank, it's Leilani. Angel can't come to the phone; he's sitting on Peter Brentwood. He broke into my apartment."

"Glad to hear it," Hank said. "Swede just located footage of the man breaking into your storage shed at the marina last night during the time Dev reported the party noise on the two yachts."

Leilani glared at the man squirming beneath Angel. She'd never allowed herself to hate anyone until now. "So, he was the one who tampered with the speargun?"

"Reid had the Maui Police dust the shed for prints. Now that Brentwood has committed the crime of breaking and entering your apartment, they'll take his fingerprints and match them to those on the lock and the speargun."

"If he didn't wipe down the surfaces like he did on the boat," she pointed out.

"He wasn't wearing gloves and ended up leaving quickly because the party on the yacht was spreading out."

"The bastard deserves to rot in jail" Leilani said through gritted teeth. "He almost killed my cousin."

"So, we heard," Hank said. "We're glad he came through surgery all right."

"Swede also did some digging into Brentwood's credit cards and found an Uber charge from a pickup near that beach where the jet boat was abandoned and to the harbor where it was stolen in the first place. He reviewed video footage from earlier that day and found images of a man leaving the harbor in the jet boat. He backed up to a few minutes earlier and found the same man leaning against one of the buildings close enough that the camera caught his face. It was Brentwood."

"You've got nothing on me," Brentwood ground out. "So, I had an Uber charge. I have them often. I was visiting a friend that day, and I took an Uber. It proves nothing. That's how a lot of people get around on Maui."

"Yet, you were caught in my apartment uninvited," Leilani said. "It's not looking good for you, Mr. Brentwood."

"Look, I came to present the latest and final offer from my client."

"And you just invited yourself in to wait for me to return?" Leilani snorted. "And how did you get inside without a key?"

"The police will be here in ten minutes," Reid said. "Wanna bring him into Leilani's apartment?"

Angel's brow formed into a V over his nose. "Not really, but yeah."

Between the three men, they half-carried, half-dragged the man toward Leilani's suite.

As soon as Leilani stepped through the door, she gasped.

Bright red paint had been sprayed across the walls, with the message *NO MORE TOURS.*

"It's just paint," Angel said as they maneuvered the man through the doorway into Leilani's apartment. "Got any zip ties?"

"Sorry," Leilani said. "No zip ties. However, I have a scarf you can use to secure his wrists. I'll get it."

Leilani ducked into her bedroom and grabbed the scarf off a shelf in the tiny closet. She hurried back to Angel and handed over the pretty scarf she'd never actually worn.

Angel worked quickly, tying the scarf around Brentwood's wrists. Once the man was secured,

Angel rose to his feet, leaving the broker struggling to sit up.

When he did, he glared at Leilani.

"Why did you do this to me?" she asked him.

"You should've taken the offer," Brentwood said.

She shook her head. "And you thought terrorizing me and my employees would wear me down?"

"The money would've set you up for the rest of your life if you invested it wisely. You're a fool to hold onto that land."

"It belongs to me and my father before me, and his father before him and his father before him. I would never sell it."

"You say never, but when you have no money and limited access to making more, you will sell to survive." Brentwood's lip curled back.

"Speaking from experience?" Leilani quipped.

Brentwood snorted. "Damn right."

"*Your* choices determine *your* trajectory," Leilani said. "And your trajectory is headed straight for jail."

A police officer entered Leilani's suite. "Got a call about a breaking and entering suspect?"

"You're in the right place," Leilani told the officer about the man breaking into her room, then running away to escape, and who was subsequently caught.

The officer listened to Angel's account as well before he led Brentwood out to his car with Reid and Teller as his escort.

After the police officer left with Brentwood,

Leilani remembered she'd been on the phone with Hank. "You still there?" she asked.

"I am," Hank responded. "Sounds like you caught your guy."

Leilani looked around the room and realized for the first time that it was over. "We did," she breathed and sank onto the sofa. "It was Peter Brentwood. The police just hauled him off."

"You should rest easier tonight," Hank said. "And you can get your tour business up and running again."

"I can," she said. "Thank you, Hank. And thank Swede for me."

"I will," he said.

"I can't believe he did it all for money." Leilani shook her head.

"His ex-wife took everything," Hank said. "He was probably pretty desperate."

"He almost killed my cousin."

"I heard he made it through surgery all right," Hank said.

"He did." Leilani was thankful her cousin survived.

"Let me know if you need anything else," Hank said. "I'll have Swede forward everything he found on the video surveillance systems to the Maui Police. In the meantime, get some rest. Tomorrow is a new day full of potential."

Leilani ended the call and looked up to find everyone had left except Angel. "It's over, she said.

He held open his arms,

Leilani threw herself into them. The danger was past. Which meant she wouldn't need twenty-four-seven protection.

"You'll be leaving soon," she said softly.

"Not until the end of the week," he said. "Unless you want me to move out now."

She clung to him. "No. I want you to stay." *Forever.*

But Angel had a job to go to on the Big Island.

And Leilani had a business to rebuild on Maui. Yeah, she'd thought for a moment about selling everything and moving on.

Her afternoon with Angel exploring Maui had reminded her of how much she loved her home.

On the other hand, if she sold everything, she could be open to moving around. She could go to the Big Island and potentially be with Angel.

With Angel's departure from Maui looming, Leilani refused to waste a single minute.

She was so close to one hundred percent. She wasn't ready to give up, nor was she ready to let go.

She just hoped Angel felt the same.

CHAPTER 14

THE NEXT FEW days passed in a busy haze for Leilani. Not far from her thoughts was Angel's pending departure. His days on Maui were coming to an end.

On the last night of his stay, Leilani took him and his three friends to an event she couldn't get out of and didn't want to. She'd been looking forward to this party for a month. It was to be a reunion of people from Lahaina, bringing together those who were still on Maui who'd been displaced when they'd lost their homes.

Leilani couldn't wait to see old friends she hadn't spoken to in months. There would be traditional Hawaiian music and dancing, as well as a DJ for later in the evening.

Kiana had helped her find another dress in the lost and found. This one was a beautiful tropical print, strapless dress that hugged her breasts and hips, the hem stopping at mid-thigh, exposing her knees and calves and making her legs appear longer.

She'd pulled her hair up into a messy bun on top of her head, leaving long tendrils loose around her ears.

When she stepped out of the bathroom, Angel let out a long, low whistle. "Wow," he said. "I like this dress even more than the white one. It showcases your Hawaiian features."

She smiled. "That's what I loved most about it. I feel like it's me, ready to celebrate." She leaned up on her toes and kissed him. "I can't think of anyone I'd rather celebrate with than you."

"Same." He kissed her back, then looked around. "Got your purse and phone?"

Kiana had loaned her a crossbody purse in a sparkling silver with a silver chain strap. She started to put her phone in the purse, but Angel laid his hand over hers holding the phone. "This is my last night on Maui. I don't know exactly what will happen when I report to our headquarters on the Big Island, but I'd like to know you're okay when I can't be with you."

She frowned up at him. "We can always text."

"I want you to have my phone location. That way, you'll know where I am. I always have my phone with me."

"I'd like that." She held up her cell phone. "Do you want to be able to track my phone location?"

His lips widened into a grin. "I was hoping you'd offer. I didn't want to come off as a stalker."

Her cheeks heated. "I like knowing you can find me wherever I am. It will make me feel like you're still with me. How do we share our locations?"

He pulled out his phone. They spent a few minutes changing their settings to allow each other to find their phones wherever they were.

Angel brought up the app that displayed a pin for each of their phones. "See? We're together on the map."

She nodded. "I like that."

He pulled her to him. "I like that you like that. And if you ever are uncomfortable sharing your location with me, you know how to turn it off."

"As do you." Her gut twisted. "You might find a new girlfriend. She might not want you tracking the old one."

He took her hands in his. "I don't want another girlfriend. The way I see it, Maui brought us together when she made you slip on that trail. I'll be back. I just don't know when."

She looked up into his eyes, her heart full. "Ninety-nine."

"I need to up my game," he said and kissed her so thoroughly that her head spun, and her knees turned to jelly.

When he finally raised his head, she clung to him.

"Keep that up, and we won't make it out of this room."

"Challenge accepted." He lowered his head to kiss her again.

Before his lips touched hers, a knock sounded on the door to Leilani's suite.

Angel sighed, brushed his mouth lightly over hers and stepped back. "We're being summoned."

Leilani laughed and hurried past him to open the door.

Olina stood there with her three children. "Tell me the truth...do I look all right?" She wore a sleeveless sundress in a bright red, pink and orange pattern that perfectly complimented her dark skin.

Leilani hugged her friend. "You're adorable." She looked past Olina to the children, all wearing shorts, T-shirts and tennis shoes. "Are you ready for the Lahaina Olympics?"

All three children shouted, "Yes!"

Noa reached for Angel's hand. "I want to do the three-legged race, but no one will do it with me. Will you, Mr. Angelo?"

Angel knelt to get on eye-level with the five-year-old. "I'd be honored to race with you."

Noa's smile lit his face. "We're going to win!"

Angel laughed and straightened. "I don't know about that, but we're going to do our best."

"You sure you don't mind that I'm taking your car?" Olina asked.

"Not at all," Leilani said. "But after tomorrow, we'll have to juggle our schedules again."

Olina's eyes widened. "That's right." She looked at Angel. "You're leaving. We'll miss you." Her gaze shot to Leilani. "Are you going to be all right?"

Leilani forced a smile because crying on a day of celebration wasn't cool. "I will."

"Let's get moving," Angel said. "The guys are following us to the event location."

They met Dev, Reid and Teller in the parking lot and piled into three vehicles. Angel and Leilani led the way in the first car, and the others fell in behind them. In twenty minutes, they pulled into the parking lot of a park with a large pavilion lined with picnic tables and several tents with different foods offered for an early dinner. After they ate, a three-person band played traditional Hawaiian music while two women wearing colorful dresses and flower leis performed the hula dance.

During a pause between activities, several people gave updates on the cleanup effort in Lahaina and shared information about timelines and agencies they could contact for assistance. By the time announcements were done, the children were restless, ready to start the Lahaina version of the Olympics.

Dev, Reid and Teller had found the beer tent and were ensconced in folding chairs, talking with other men, probably swapping war stories.

Leilani was glad the men were having fun on the last night of their vacation.

Olina stood with the mothers of her children's friends, catching up on where they were and how the children were doing in their temporary schools.

Mamo and Palili participated in running an obstacle course set up with a low balance beam, rope ladder, rope swing, culvert pipe and old tires to run through. They were winded and laughing when they finished.

The sun sank low on the horizon when they called for contestants for the three-legged race. Noa grabbed Angel's hand and dragged him to the starting line.

Leilani positioned herself near the finish line and watched as the officials tied Noa's small leg to one of Angel's. The height difference was adorable.

"He'll make a good father," a voice said beside her.

Leilani turned to find Alyssa beside her, wearing a pretty red dress with a wide skirt falling to mid-calf. She looked like a model about to stride down a runway. She held two red plastic cups. Immediately, Leilani tensed, remembering how angry Alyssa had been the last time she'd seen her the day of Makai's surgery.

"I want to apologize for my bad behavior the other day. As an olive branch, I brought you a Mai Tai. I hope you can find room in your heart to forgive me for all the hateful things I said." She held out the cup.

Leilani hesitated a moment before she took the offering. "What hurts most is that you believe those things about me, or you wouldn't have said them."

"I was frightened, scared of losing Makai and so very wrong. You mean a lot to Makai. Makai means a lot to me. Therefore, you mean a lot to me by default."

Leilani's lips tightened. "I don't want to be a default to anyone."

"I'm not very good at this," Alyssa said, shaking her head. "What I'm trying to say is that I'm sorry, and I want us to be friends. If not now, eventually. I'll prove to you that I can be nice and not yell at you unprovoked." She gave a tremulous smile and held up her cup. "To second chances?"

One of Leilani's faults was that she couldn't stay mad long. It wasn't in her nature. Though she wasn't ready to accept Alyssa's apology, she raised her cup for her cousin. He'd want her to get along with his future bride. Leilani wanted Makai to be happy. "To second chances," she touched the rim of her cup to Alyssa's and then downed half the drink, enjoying the icy coolness sliding down her throat.

The race had yet to begin. One official struggled to tie the knot around a little boy's leg and his mother's. The child appeared to be a moving target, holding everyone else up.

Leilani drank more of her fruity drink, finishing it. Still, the race hadn't started.

She'd been standing for what felt like hours and would like to have found a seat. The temperature seemed to be getting hotter, not cooler, with the sun setting on the horizon.

"Is it hot out here, or is it me?" Leilani fanned herself with her empty hand.

"It is a little warmer than usual," Alyssa said. "Your face a little flushed. Are you feeling all right?"

Leilani looked toward Angel and Noa at the starting line, and her vision blurred. "I don't know," she said. "I'm not feeling well."

"You need to sit down." Alyssa hooked her arm. "Let me help you." Instead of guiding her over to the picnic tables in the pavilion, Alyssa led her to the parking lot.

"There are seats in the pavilion," Leilani said, feeling too woozy to get anywhere on her own.

"You need a seat with air conditioning. Come sit in my car. I'll crank up the AC. You'll feel better in no time."

"I need to watch the race," Leilani said. Her words slurred along with her vision. At this point, she just wanted to lay on the ground until the world stopped spinning. "What's wrong with me?"

"Nothing a little air-conditioning won't fix," Alyssa said and slipped her arm around Leilani, supporting more of her weight as Leilani's legs were too wobbly to hold her up.

When they reached Alyssa's Jeep, she opened the door and helped Leilani into the passenger seat. "See? Better already."

Leilani wasn't so sure about that. She struggled to locate the lever on the seat that would allow her to recline. When her fingers grasped it, she could barely make it turn. When it did, she fell backward.

Alyssa climbed into the driver's seat, started the engine and turned the air conditioner up to full blast. "That's right. Take a nap. You'll feel better. In a few minutes, it'll all be over."

"What will be over?" Leilani said, though her words didn't sound right. She closed her eyes to keep the world from whirling around her.

She must have passed out because when she opened her eyes, Alyssa was standing beside her in the door of the Jeep, reaching beneath Leilani's arms. "Come on, Leilani, I have a surprise for you."

Leilani could barely lift her head. She didn't want a surprise. She wanted to go home to bed with Angel.

"Where's Angel?" she whispered.

"He's waiting for you at the boat. That's the surprise. He wanted to have a quiet dinner on the Windsong II with you. I think he's going to propose. Come on. You don't want to miss it."

"Can't move."

"You have to. He's waiting." Alyssa's jaw set as she

lifted Leilani from her seat and dragged her from the Jeep.

Leilani managed to get her feet on the ground and stand for a moment before her legs buckled, and she fell.

Alyssa caught her in a chair.

Leilani's head lolled to the side as she slumped in the chair, her nose almost bumping into a wheel.

"Like your ride?" Alyssa propped Leilani's feet on the metal foot flaps. "I borrowed this wheelchair from Makai. He's not up to using it yet. It'll be a long time before he can get around. Thanks to you."

The woman was behind her now, pushing her across a parking lot toward the marina.

Leilani couldn't comprehend what was going on and was too weak to do anything about it.

When they reached the dock, Alyssa kept going, pushing the wheelchair past a line of boats, standing eerily empty, the shadows around them swirling in Leilani's vision.

Alyssa came to a halt next to a boat.

Leilani managed to tip her head to the other side, the name of the boat coming into view. "That's my boat," she said, her words slurring like she was drunk. She'd only had one drink. She couldn't be drunk. It didn't make sense. Nothing made sense. "I need to lay down."

"You can do that as soon as we get you on board.

Then you can sleep until your man gets here for your surprise."

"Want to go back."

"Sorry," Alyssa said, her voice hardening. "There's no going back. Now, get on the boat."

Alyssa rounded to the front of the wheelchair and moved Leilani's feet off the metal flaps. "Come on. On your feet." Alyssa grabbed Leilani's hand, yanked her up and out of the chair, then staggered backward under her weight. She spun and angled Leilani toward the boat, then gave her a big shove.

Leilani fell onto the deck, landing so hard the air was knocked out of her lungs. She lay still, trying to breathe and failing.

For a long moment, she thought she would die. That she'd never know what surprise Angel had planned for her.

Alyssa disappeared.

Leilani lay with her cheek pressed to the cool deck. She must have blacked out again because the next thing she knew, Alyssa was back, and she was pouring something from a big jug onto the deck.

The acrid scent of fuel assailed Leilani's nostrils. Was Alyssa pouring gas into the boat's tank? If so, she was missing horribly, spilling it all over the deck.

Then she set the jug down beside her and pulled what looked like a box of matches out of her pocket.

Leilani tried to tell her it was dangerous to light a match around gasoline. "What are you doing?"

Alyssa laughed. "The only thing I can do to fix what you destroyed." She pulled a match out of the box and struck the tip against the side. The match flared, but a breeze kicked up extinguishing the flame.

Leilani tried and failed to lift her head from where it lay against the deck. "I don't understand."

"You ruined Makai and my chances to win the competition at the Eddie. Had we been able to participate, we would've won the contest and landed a number of lucrative endorsements for the cute couple who surfs together. I had it all lined up. All we had to do was get there and surf our best." She lit another match. The breeze blew that one out as well.

"We could've paid off all our debt and had money coming in from the endorsements. But you just couldn't let go of anything. You should've sold when Brentwood first came to you with the contract. He wouldn't have sabotaged your business to force you into bankruptcy and make you sell your property in Lahaina."

"What are you talking about?" She wasn't making sense.

"Makai wouldn't have felt bad about what Brentwood was doing to you and gone to bail you out. He wouldn't have taken that damned spear in his leg. He'd be with me at the Eddie." She swiped another match against the box. It lit, and she flung it at the gasoline on the deck. "Now, we have nothing but debt. The only way we can dig our way out is for you to die!" The match ignited the fuel and spread so fast the entire deck was in flames in seconds, except for where Leilani lay in the middle and Alyssa stood by the stern.

Heat built around Leilani, taking her back to her escape from Lahaina.

"No," she said, dragging herself across the deck toward Alyssa. "You won't fix anything if I die."

"I will," Alyssa said, her voice getting higher, tighter as she lifted the jug of gasoline and shook it at the growing flames. "Makai's your only living relative. He'll inherit your property. We'll sell it and use that money to pay off our debt, buy a house on Oahu and get the hell away from this dead-end island."

"Makai won't inherit," Leilani said.

Alyssa wasn't listening. She shook out more fuel. It splashed into the flames and onto the floor at her feet. Some landed on her skirt. The next time she flung fuel on the fire, the flames followed the stream back to the jug.

Alyssa dropped the jug. More fuel spilled onto her dress. The flames leaped toward her, caught on her dress and flared. Alyssa screamed and slapped at the flames, but they quickly spread across the highly flammable fabric and caught in her hair. Instead of jumping into the water to extinguish the fire, she leaped onto the dock and ran as if trying to escape the pain.

Leilani was surrounded by flames. She turned as best she could, searching for a gap, her body so heavy she could barely make it move. Behind her, the fire had consumed the fuel in one spot and had yet to ignite the decking.

Leilani half-crawled, half-dragged herself through the gap to the starboard side. Grabbing onto the hook that held the donut-shaped life preserver, she used every ounce of her waning strength and pulled herself to her feet. Her entire body shook with the effort.

She had to get into the water.

By now, the fire had eaten into the decking and was spreading toward her.

She pulled the life ring free and dropped it over the side of the boat.

As flames surged toward her, she leaned over the side and let gravity do the rest.

CHAPTER 15

ANGEL AND NOA won the three-legged race. The boy was so excited he hugged Angel's neck for a full five minutes. Then, he dragged his competition partner over to share their win with his mother.

Angel looked for Leilani. She'd said she'd wait at the finish line. He'd seen her standing there when they'd been waiting to have their legs tied together. At one point, a woman in a red dress had joined her. That was when the wild kid caused a commotion, drawing everyone's attention while the officials and the kid's mother struggled to get him to stand still long enough to have the rope tied to his leg. Once they were ready, the officials had them line up, the whistle was blown, and they were off and running.

He and Noa had tripped a couple of times, managing to right themselves and continue forward until they crossed the finish line first.

"Have you seen Leilani?" he asked Olina.

Olina frowned, looking around. "Not since before the race."

"If you see her, let her know I'm looking for her." Angel waded through the crowd, looking for her petite form, afraid that because she was so short, he might be missing her.

When he came to where Dev, Reid and Teller were sitting, he was frowning in earnest.

"What's wrong? Did you lose the race?" Dev asked.

He shook his head, still looking around. "We won. Have you seen Leilani?"

"Not since dinner," Reid said.

"Is she carrying her cell phone?" Teller asked.

"Yes."

"Call her," Teller said at the same time as the thought came to Angel.

He selected her number from his contact list and placed the call. It rang five times and rolled over to her voicemail. His frown deepened.

"Not answering?" Reid asked. "She might be in the bathroom."

Angel brought up his finder app. His location was correct. He expected Leilani's to come up with his. It didn't. "What the hell?"

"What's wrong?" Dev asked.

"Her phone shows her at the Maalaea Harbor." He looked up. "Did she tell any of you she was going there?"

All three men shook their heads as one.

"She wouldn't have gone without telling me." His gut twisted. "I have a bad feeling." Angel spun and headed for his car.

His three friends were on their feet in seconds, quickly catching up.

Angel jumped into the driver's seat and cranked the engine. He was backing out as the other three were piling in.

He handed his cell phone to Reid in the passenger seat and focused on the road, breaking every speed limit between the park and the harbor. When he pulled into the parking lot ten minutes later, his heart sank to his knees. Flames licked the sky from one of the boats moored on the dock.

Angel shoved the shift into park and flew out of the car, racing toward the burning boat, knowing in his gut that Leilani was on it.

When he reached the dock, a figure jumped off the flaming boat engulfed in flame, a human torch hurtling toward him.

Angel's heart burned. "Leilani!" He ran toward her but realized this burning person was too tall to be Leilani. What was left of her charred hair was blond, not dark brown.

She screamed like an animal in pain and flung herself at Angel.

Reid stepped in front of Angel, bare-chested.

Holding his shirt in front of himself, he caught the woman and wrapped the shirt around her. "Go! Find Leilani!" he yelled as he patted the flames in an attempt to extinguish the fire.

Angel was already running. When he reached the boat, it was completely engulfed in flames, the fire so hot he couldn't get close. "Leilani!" he yelled. He yanked his shirt over his head, wrapped it around his arms and pressed it to his mouth and nose. He sucked in a deep breath and lunged toward the boat.

Hands caught him on either side, yanking him back onto the dock.

"You can't get on that boat," Dev said. "If she's on it, she won't be alive."

"We need to get back." Teller tugged on Angel's arm. "When the fire reaches the gas tank, it'll blow."

Angel shrugged him off. "No. She can't be on that boat. She can't be dead. Leilani survived one fire; she can't die in this one." He tried to think. "What would Leilani do?" Then it came to him. "The water. Look in the water!" He ran to the starboard side of the boat and peered into the inky black water that reflected the orange flames rising into the air.

Orange flames. Something orange floated near the side of the boat. At first, he thought it was more reflections of the flames. But it wasn't flickering. The edges were rounded.

Angel dove into the water and swam toward the

orange object. As he neared it, the heat from the burning boat became more intense.

The object was a life preserver. He looked around, desperate now. The gas tank on board could blow at any moment. "Leilani!"

A hand rose from the far side of the orange life preserver. "Angel?"

Angel pulled the floatation device toward him and spun it slowly.

Leilani had looped her arm through the rope on the preserver. Her head leaned against it, her nose barely above the water.

"Oh, baby. How did I let this happen?" Angel untangled her arm and looped his arm over her shoulder, his hand hooking beneath the opposite arm. Leaning back, he swam the sidestroke, cleaving through the water to put as much distance as he could between them and the burning boat.

"There they are!" Dev and Teller ran along the dock, keeping pace with Angel until he was far enough away from the boat that they'd be safe if it exploded. Then he swam toward the dock to a ladder.

Dev shimmied down the rickety ladder and reached for Leilani. While he pulled, Angel pushed until Teller could grab hold of her and bring her up onto the dock. Teller gathered Leilani in his arms and headed for the parking lot.

Dev and Angel caught up to him as they converged on Reid, where he knelt beside the woman who'd been on fire moments before. "She's dead," Reid said, staring down at her. "I could be wrong, but I think it was—"

"Alyssa," Leilani said, her voice barely above a whisper.

"We have to get out of here," Dev said. "If that boat blows, it could set off a chain reaction with the boats moored on either side of it."

"Let me have her," Angel said, reaching for Leilani.

Teller transferred her into Angel's arms.

Reid lifted Alyssa into his arms.

They hurried off the dock and ran for the parking lot.

They'd made it as far as the line of sheds when an explosion ripped through the air.

Angel dropped to his knees and used his body to shield Leilani.

Another explosion followed shortly after.

"I think we're far enough away," Teller said. "Let's get to the car."

At the car, Angel dropped to the ground, pulled Leilani into his arms and rocked her, his body shaking. "Babe, I think I lost ten years off my life."

Leilani stared up at him. "You and me both." Her words were breathy and slurred.

"How did she get you here?"

"Drugged." Leilani closed her eyes. "Can we go home now?"

"The fire department and an ambulance are on the way," Dev reported.

Reid laid Alyssa's body on the ground.

Leilani's head tilted toward the woman. "She thought that if I died, Makai would inherit the land as my only living relative. She didn't know." Leilani looked up at Angel. "If I die with no direct descendants, the land goes to the state of Hawaii."

Angel hugged her close. "I'm glad you didn't die. You mean too much to me."

Her lips curled in a soft smile. "I wasn't going to die. Especially not in a fire." She lay quietly for a moment. "Not when I'm one hundred percent, crazy in love with you, and I haven't had the chance to tell you. If you're not one hundred percent, that's okay. I can wait. But I wanted you to know in case it makes a difference."

"Babe, it makes a difference. I don't want to go another day without telling you how I feel."

"And how is that?" she asked softly.

He laid a hand over his heart. "One hundred percent."

EPILOGUE

Two weeks later

Kiana hugged Leilani's neck. "I can't believe you're moving out. I got used to having you close."

Leilani smiled. "I'm going to miss having coffee with you in the morning. But I'll make sure I come by once a week on my way to the dock. Or I'll do the land tour and come early so we can catch up on gossip. Either way, I'm not going that far away. Just up in the hills. Angel's boss has connections with the owners of the Parkman Ranch on the Big Island. They have a wealthy friend who keeps a house here on Maui and is rarely here. He offered to let me and Angel live there until we can rebuild in Lahaina. I can even have Makai move in with me when he's ready."

"I'm glad to hear that," Kiana said. "I was worried about how he's been since Alyssa's death. He doesn't have anyone to help him when he's released from rehab."

"I asked him if he wanted to move in now. We could hire someone to help him until he can help himself."

Kiana's brow dipped. "He didn't jump at the chance to leave the rehab facility?"

Leilani shook her head. "That shocked me, too, until I saw his physical therapist. She's hot and into surfers but doesn't surf."

"Perfect," Kiana sighed. "I have to admit, I'm jealous." She shot a glance toward Angel as he loaded Leilani's belongings into the car he'd purchased.

Leilani's eyebrows rose. "Kiana. Seriously. Do you have a thing for my man?"

Kiana laughed. "No. I'm not in the market for a relationship. I only pick the bad ones. It's better if I don't pick one at all." She gave her friend a crooked smile. "I'm jealous you found love. I'd begun to think it doesn't exist."

"You'll find the right one for you," Leilani said, "when you least expect it."

"Oh, please. I like being single. I don't have to answer to anyone, I don't have to worry that my significant other is stealing my money, and I can date whoever I want, whenever I want."

Dev appeared, carrying a box full of Leilani's computer parts and cords. "Did I hear you want to date? I'm single and available. I'd go out with you."

Kiana rolled her eyes. "My standards might be too high for you."

Dev chuckled. "Try me."

Kiana raised a finger. "Number one: Are you employed?"

He laid the box in the trunk of the car Angel had been packing. "Employed? Check. Brotherhood Protectors. You can call my boss. He'll vouch for me."

Leilani grinned. "He doesn't know who he's up against," she murmured as Angel came to stand beside her.

"Dev's a man who can't take no for an answer. No woman has ever turned him down."

"Until Kiana," Leilani said.

"Wanna put money on that?" Angel said.

Leilani's lips twisted into a cocky smile. "Ten bucks says she'll shoot him down."

"Fifty bucks says she'll say yes." Angel held out a hand.

"You're on." Leilani gripped his hand and gave it a firm shake.

Kiana was up to number three. Number two being *Are you a mama's boy*? No. Three: Ever declared bankruptcy? No.

"Do you have any children from a previous marriage or relationship?" Kiana asked.

"No," Dev answered.

She tilted her head, her eyes narrowing. "No, you don't, or not that you know of?"

"No, I don't. I use protection like a religion." He crossed his arms over his chest. "What else ya got?"

"Ever broken up with a girl over a text message?"

"No. Always in person," his lips twitched. "Even if she's batshit crazy and might scratch my eyes out or leave me permanently scarred."

Kiana's brow rose. "Did one try to scratch your eyes out?"

He shrugged. "Tried. I deflected her killer nails." Dev pulled back his sleeve to reveal a long, thick scar. "She missed my eyes but got my arm."

"How do you feel about kids?" Kiana asked.

"Love them," he said.

"Oh, he's treading on thin ground now," Leilani whispered.

Angel chuckled. "He's got this, I tell you."

"I love them," Dev repeated, "As long as I can give them back."

Kiana nodded slowly. "Marriage? For or against?"

"For," Dev answered.

Leilani made a motion like a plane being shot down.

Angel held up a hand. "Wait for it."

"I'm all for other people getting married. It's just not for me."

Angel grinned down at Leilani.

"Oh, he's good," she said.

"Always gets his gal," Angel said.

Kiana crossed her arms over her chest like Dev. "Final question. Favorite position?"

Dev tipped his head as if giving the question a lot of consideration. "Whatever position brings my partner the greatest pleasure."

"Mmm," Leilani said. "At this point, I'd go out with him."

Angel frowned. "The hell you will. Have I ever disappointed?"

She laughed, leaned up on her toes and kissed him. "Never." She turned her attention back to Kiana. "Here comes the finale."

"So," Dev stepped toward Kiana. "Did I pass your test?"

"Yes, you did."

"Great. I can pick you up at six."

Leilani held out her hand. "Fifty bucks."

Angel's eyebrows drew together in confusion. "He passed her test."

Kiana shook her head. "Not so fast."

"Huh?" Angel frowned.

"So, you're not going out with me?" Dev said.

Kiana shook her head. "Nope."

"Why not?"

She flipped her long blond hair over her shoulder. "You never actually asked. You assumed." Kiana leaned close and laid a hand on his chest. "That's too bad. I was hoping you could show me yours, and I could show you mine."

Dev licked his lips. "Show your what?"

"Positions," she said. "Mine are really kinky." Kiana winked. "Better luck next woman."

Angel pulled out his wallet and dropped fifty dollars into Leilani's hand.

As she walked away, Kiana's cell phone rang. She pulled it out of her pocket and frowned at the screen before pressing the phone to her ear. "Tish? What's wrong?"

Leilani frowned. "That's not good."

"What's not good?" Angel said. "Who's Tish?"

"Tish was one of her roommates in Honolulu, back when she was modeling."

"Kiana's a model?" Angel stared at the resort manager.

Dev joined them. "I can see it. She's stunning."

"And she shot you down, costing me fifty bucks," Angel grumbled.

Dev grinned. "I'm not crying. But then I didn't lose fifty bucks."

Kiana walked several steps away, listening for a moment. "She's probably just hooked up with some guy." Listening again. "That long? Missed a call? That's not like her. Not even for a guy." Kiana sighed. "Don't freak out. I'll take time off and hop a plane in the morning. We'll find her. See you tomorrow, Tish. Yeah, I remember. Friends forever." Kiana ended the call and stood with her back to them for a few more moments.

When she turned, she walked toward Leilani and hugged her tight. "Love you, Lani. I might be out of pocket for a few days. I have some business to take care of in Honolulu."

Leilani touched her friend's arm. "That was Tish, wasn't it? What's wrong?"

Kiana shook her head. "Nothing you need to worry about. You have enough on your plate."

Leilani frowned. "Honolulu can be dangerous. You know that."

Kiana nodded. "I do. It's why I left."

"Is Tish in trouble?" Leilani asked.

"No." Kiana sighed. "Meredith didn't come home to the apartment."

"Last night?" Leilani pressed.

"No," Kiana's lips pressed into a thin line. "Last week. She doesn't usually disappear for that long. I'm worried she took some escort gigs to fill the gaps between modeling jobs."

"Kiana," Leilani grabbed her hand. "Call the cops. Some of those clients are dangerous."

"Yeah. Even more of a reason for me to go. Meredith is too gullible and naïve to be an escort."

"You can't go alone," Leilani said. "I—"

Angel stepped forward. "Don't say it."

Leilani frowned at Angel. "Don't say what?"

"You can't go with her. From the way it sounds, Kiana needs protection."

Leilani cocked an eyebrow. "If you'd let me finish,

I was going to say that I think she needs protection. Someone from the Brotherhood Protectors. That's what they do."

Kiana frowned. "I can't step back into that life with a hulking bodyguard. A hulking pimp, maybe, but not a bodyguard. They'll get suspicious right off the bat. Then they'll clam up, and I won't get any information about anyone."

"You need a good-looking guy who can charm people into telling their deepest, darkest secrets," Dev suggested.

Kiana's eyebrows twisted. "Got one in mind?"

Dev poked a thumb at his chest. "Me."

Kiana's eyes narrowed. For a long moment, she stared at Dev, letting her gaze sweep over him from the top of his perfect hair to his designer shoes.

"Yeah, you might do," she finally said. "Can you be ready at six?"

"That was my line," he said with a grin.

"In the morning," she said, arching a brow. "This is not a date. I'd be hiring you to protect me and help me look for Meredith."

"That's what we do," Dev said.

"I don't need a date. I don't want a relationship. I'm not going to fall in love with you," she said. "I'd appreciate it if you'd refrain from hitting on me, calling me sweetheart, and for God's sake, don't fancy yourself falling in love with me."

He popped a salute. "Yes, ma'am."

Kiana rolled her eyes. "And never call me ma'am."

"Yes, ma'am...Kiana." He grinned. "Looks like you've just hired a Brotherhood Protector."

Kiana pinned him with a fierce stare. "Don't make me regret it."

KIANA'S HERO

BROTHERHOOD PROTECTORS HAWAII
BOOK #3

New York Times & USA Today
Bestselling Author

ELLE JAMES

Kiana's

HERO

BROTHERHOOD PROTECTORS HAWAII

New York Times & USA Today Bestselling Author

ELLE JAMES

ABOUT KIANA'S HERO

Former Marine Force Recon, Devlin Mulhaney left the military when politics interfered with the mission, and he lost a friend. He quickly realizes that civilian life can prove to be just as dangerous.

When her high-class fiancé absconded with all the money she'd worked so hard to accumulate, fashion model, Kiana Williams, left the catwalk in Honolulu and disappeared to Maui to start a new life in a less dangerous field. A call from a former roommate drags her back to search for a missing friend. This time, she's not going in alone. She hires Brotherhood Protectors' Dev Mulhaney to ensure her safety and to help her locate her missing friend. Her conditions:

I don't need a date.
I don't want a relationship.
I'm not going to fall in love with you.

Together they navigate a growing attraction in the midst of the dangerous world of high fashion and elite escorts, where money can buy beautiful things or get you killed.

CHAPTER 1

KIANA WILLIAMS LEANED her head back against the thin seat of the commuter plane that would carry her and Devlin Mulhaney from the Hawaiian island of Maui to Oahu. Flight time was less than forty minutes from wheels up to wheels down. She closed her eyes in an attempt to discourage conversation with the man. "Thank you for being on time to catch our flight this morning."

"My pleasure," he said, his tone low, sexy and too much for that early.

A shiver of awareness rippled across her skin.

"Since I'm here to protect you and, potentially, your friend, you should bring me up to speed on her —where she lives, what she does for a living, and anything else I might need to know."

Kiana's lips pressed into a thin line. "You're

supposed to be the expert protector. I would think you could react to any situation."

He chuckled. "I'm not a mind-reader. As a former Marine Force Reconnaissance operator, I am combat trained; however, you can never have too much information about your opponent or the situation. We never went in blind unless we absolutely had no other choice."

She sighed. "Fair enough." Without lifting her head, she told him what she knew, which wasn't much. She'd been up through the night worried about her friend and former roommate, trying to guess what could have happened. Every potential scenario she came up with was increasingly horrible, giving her a bad feeling in the pit of her belly.

Kiana opened her eyes and sat up straight. "My friend and former roommate, Meredith O'Neil, shares an apartment with my other friend, Tish Brinks. As you know, Tish called yesterday to say Meredith was missing." Dev had been there when she'd gotten the call. "Normally, I wouldn't be too worried. Meredith has been known to stay a night or two with her boyfriend. When Tish clarified Meredith had been gone for a week, that was different. Staying over with a boyfriend for a night or two was one thing; not coming home for a week is another."

"Did Tish try calling Meredith's boyfriend?" Dev asked.

Kiana grimaced. "Tish said Meredith had broken up with her boyfriend over a month ago. He's out of the picture."

"Still worth a call," Dev pointed out. "They could've gotten back together."

Kiana nodded. "Tish called. No answer. The last she'd heard from Meredith was that she was taking an escort job to help make rent money. Apparently, that was the night she disappeared, as far as Tish could tell. Meredith hadn't texted to say she was staying the night with a friend, a man or anyone else."

Dev frowned. "An escort job? What do you mean?"

Kiana glanced at Dev, her brow wrinkling. "It's like going on a date with someone, only you get paid."

"That could be dicey," Dev said.

Kiana's brow dipped. "It's not prostitution."

Dev gave her half a smile. "I didn't say it was."

Kiana had the sudden urge to defend her friend and the profession of paid escorts. "Usually, it's a businessman wanting someone to attend a corporate function with him, or a wealthy man who just wants someone to eat dinner with him, rather than sitting at a table by himself."

"Do the clients expect more?"

"Some do," Kiana admitted. "Before an escort is assigned, the escort service explains the rules and emphasizes the service isn't for sex. It's up to the escort to state upfront about what she expects and her limits to reinforce what the service already told them."

Dev met and held her gaze. "How often does the client push for more?"

Kiana looked away. "If the escort states the ground rules, the client usually abides by them."

"What percentage of the time?" he persisted.

Kiana's gut clenched. "About fifty percent of the time."

"And you know this because…" he asked, his voice quiet, carrying only to her over the roar of the jet engines.

Kiana's lips curled into a tight smile as she turned to meet his gaze. "I used to work as an escort. When modeling jobs weren't plentiful, we had to make money for food, gas and rent." She lifted her chin, daring him to make a disparaging comment about being an escort. "And no. I didn't sleep with the clients. Yes, I had to fight off a few."

Dev's eyebrows dipped low. "Assholes."

She let out a short bark of laughter. "You have no idea."

He reached for her hand and gave it a quick squeeze before releasing it. "Why did Tish wait so long to call you?"

"Tish was on a modeling gig on Kauai for a couple of days and assumed Meredith had made it back from her escort assignment." Kiana's lips twisted.

"Based on the backlog of mail overflowing their mailbox and mold growing on the half-eaten bowl of cereal in the sink, Tish realized Meredith probably hadn't been back since her last message."

"Did she call the escort service?" Dev asked.

Kiana nodded. "They said they'd check into it but never got back to Tish."

"What about the police?"

"She called the police and reported Meredith as missing. I talked to Tish again last night after the police came to the apartment to ask questions. They said they'd follow up with the escort service and check in with the ex-boyfriend." Kiana wrapped her arms around her middle as a chill rippled across her body. "Tish is beside herself. She feels awful that Meredith could've been missing for a whole week, and no one has been looking for her. Don't they say the first forty-eight hours are the most important?"

Dev nodded. "Yeah. The first forty-eight hours after a crime has been committed is like the sweet spot for gathering evidence. After that, it gets harder to locate clues. They could be destroyed or thrown out with the trash. Finding people who might've seen something important to a case gets trickier."

"And memories fade the further away from the event you get." Kiana sighed. "That's what I'm afraid of."

"Why not leave it to the police to investigate?"

Dev asked. "They should have better access to information."

Kiana snorted softly. "And how many crimes are they investigating every day? A missing woman who worked as an escort might not rank high enough on their leader board, or whatever they call it." Her eyes narrowed. "The escort service might not be as open to the police with confidential client information. They'll likely wait for a search warrant."

"Which will take time to acquire." Dev's lips pressed together into a thin line.

Kiana nodded. "Time Meredith might not have. Plus, I figure the more people looking for her, the sooner we find her."

"Good point, and I'm here to help," Dev said. "We should exchange phone numbers in the unlikely event we're separated." He offered her his cell phone and held out his empty hand for hers.

Her brow furrowed as she clutched her phone to her chest.

His eyebrows rose in challenge. "It's not like I'm going to call you for a date. You made that very clear."

As she laid her phone in his palm, her fingers brushed against his skin, sending a spark of electricity shooting up her arm that shocked her in more ways than one. She grabbed his phone and quickly entered her number into his contact list, reminding herself he was her bodyguard.

Exchanging numbers was expected. Still, it felt strangely...intimate.

Once they had their own phones back, Dev slipped his into his pocket and glanced at her. "So, what's the plan?"

"First stop is the apartment. Tish might've heard back from the escort service. If she hasn't, we'll go there next." Kiana adjusted her seatbelt as the plane descended into the Honolulu International Airport.

While the plane taxied across the tarmac, Kiana called Tish.

"Are you here?" Tish answered on the first ring.

"I am." Kiana tensed at the worry in her friend's tone. "We just landed. I'll be there in less than half an hour."

"Oh, thank God," Tish said. "I don't know what else to do."

"It'll be okay," Kiana said. "We'll find her."

"I hope so," Tish said. "Hurry."

"I will." Kiana ended the call as the plane rolled to a stop. She grabbed her backpack from beneath the seat and followed Dev out.

Once in the open-air terminal, she pulled out her cell phone to arrange a lift.

Before she could request a pickup, Dev covered her hand. "I called ahead for a rental car. I figured we'd need to get around on our own without waiting for a taxi or ride-share. They'll have the keys ready. All we have to do is grab the keys and go."

Kiana's brow dipped. "You did that?"

"I did. Come on." He took her hand and led her through the airport to the rental car agency. All he had to do was give his name, and they handed over a set of keys and gave him directions to the vehicle.

Moments later, Kiana slid into the passenger seat, relieved she didn't have to wait for a ride and didn't have to do the driving in the heavy Honolulu traffic. As much as she didn't like relying on a man for anything, she was glad she had Dev with her. There was no room for stubborn independence as long as her friend was missing. She'd take all the help she could get.

And if he was handsome as hell, it wouldn't hurt to look. As long as she didn't do something stupid like fall for the guy.

She shook her head. Not a chance. Kiana had learned her lesson the hard way.

Never fall for the cute guy. He'd lie, steal your money and break your heart. Having been burned once, she refused to get that close to another flame.

"Where are we going?" Dev asked as he familiarized himself with the car's controls and started the engine.

Kiana entered an address on her smartphone and hit Go.

Between the voice on the phone and Kiana, he

was able to leave the airport and merge into the traffic heading toward Waikiki.

Kiana leaned forward in her seat, her brow knitted, one hand clenching her cell phone and the other digging into the armrest on the door.

Dev couldn't ease her worry with words. The only thing that would help would be to find her friend Meredith waiting at the apartment when they arrived. Kiana's conversation with Tish hadn't been promising. The sooner they got there, the sooner they could get started on their quest to find the missing roommate.

They left the airport, merged onto Highway 1, and soon left the highway to wind through the streets of Honolulu.

After the sixth turn, Dev slowed. "Where from here?"

Kiana laid a hand on his arm. "Stop."

Dev pressed a foot to the brake in front of a small apartment building a couple of blocks from a major road.

"Park at the rear of the building," Kiana said. "The apartment is in the back."

Dev drove around to the back of the building and found a parking space in the far corner next to a large trash bin. As soon as he shifted into Park, Kiana unclipped her seatbelt and shoved open her door.

He reached out and touched her arm. "I'm here to protect you," he said. "Let me."

She met his gaze and nodded. "Okay."

He quickly released his seatbelt and slid out of the driver's seat.

Kiana met him at the rear of the vehicle. She nodded toward the three-story building. "The apartment is on the second floor."

He took her hand, led her up the exterior metal stairs to the second floor and walked along the landing until Kiana stopped in front of the door marked 216. When she raised her hand to knock, Dev caught her arm and shook his head.

She frowned.

He touched a finger to his lips and dipped his chin toward the door, stepping between her and the knob.

The door stood ajar by barely an inch.

Kiana's eyes widened, and she stepped back behind Dev.

Stay here, he mouthed.

She nodded.

Dev pushed the door open, wishing he had an M4A1 rifle like he'd carried into urban battle in places like Iraq and Afghanistan. Either or a handgun.

As a civilian, having just gotten off an airplane and working a bodyguard-for-hire job on the island of Oahu, he was unarmed and unprepared for a major battle. All he had to rely on was his wits. No gun, no knife. Just his hands and years of experience.

The lights were off inside the apartment, which

worked for Dev and for anyone who might be lurking inside.

He eased open the door, inch by inch. Once it was wide enough for a full-grown man to enter, he hunkered low, slipped through the gap and stepped out of the wedge of light shining through behind him. Assuming a ready stance, he let his eyes adjust to the dark interior and strained to hear sounds of movement.

A pitiful feminine moan sounded from deeper inside the apartment, muffled by a wall or door. "Please…don't…I'm…not…her."

Every instinct on alert, Dev rushed toward the sound.

"No? Then where is she?" a deep, harsh voice demanded. Something loud crashed in another room.

Dev rounded a corner and raced down a short hallway with a bathroom at the end and a door on either side. The door on the right was open, the room in shambles.

A loud thud sounded as if something heavy hit the wall in the room on the left. "Tell me!" a man shouted.

Dev reached for the handle of the closed door and tried to turn it. It was locked.

"Tell me!" the man screamed. Another thud made the wall shake.

Kiana appeared beside Dev. "Oh my God. Tish?" She pounded her fist against the door.

Suspecting the man was hurting the woman, Dev grabbed Kiana and moved her away from the door. He backed far enough away and then kicked as close to the doorknob as he could.

The door frame cracked but held.

On his second kick, the frame split, and the door slammed open.

Nothing moved in the room except a filmy curtain hanging beside an open window.

A dark-haired woman lay crumpled against the wall, unmoving.

Kiana squeezed past Dev and dropped to her knees beside the woman. "Tish." She felt for a pulse. "Tish, sweetie, it's me, Kiana." Tears streamed down her cheeks. "I feel a pulse," she said. "I'm calling 911." She looked up at Dev. "Don't let him get away."

"What if he comes back?" Dev asked.

"I'm calling 911. We can't let him get away. Not after what he's done to Tish." She waved toward the window. "Either you go after him, or I will. Go!"

Dev raced for the open window and stared out.

Footsteps pounded against the landing. A man dressed in black with a black ball cap ran toward the end of the landing.

With no time to backtrack through the apartment, Dev pulled himself through the window and hit the landing running.

By that time, the assailant had reached the end of the building only to realize he'd passed the staircase leading to ground level. He turned, saw Dev heading his way and vaulted over the wrought-iron railing, dropping to the ground below.

He hit hard, rolled and staggered to his feet.

Dev didn't wait to get to the end of the landing, he braced his hands on the railing and launched himself over. When he hit the ground, he tucked and rolled as he'd learned during parachute jump school. He was on his feet in seconds, racing after the man several yards ahead of him.

The attacker moved with a decided limp, ducking through an alley and between buildings.

Dev was faster, quickly closing the distance between them.

When Dev was only two yards from catching the man, the assailant burst out of the densely packed buildings. He crossed a sidewalk, dodged between a couple of parked cars and raced out into a four-lane road.

A horn blared, tires squealed, and a huge garbage truck slammed into the man in black. The impact knocked him to the ground. The truck's front tire bumped over him before the vehicle rolled to a stop.

Dev had made it to the parked cars when he heard the horn. He was able to arrest his forward progress short of running out in front of another car. Too late to stop the inevitable, he waited until all traffic came to a complete halt.

When he was certain he wasn't going to be the

next person run over, he ran to the body lying on the pavement between the front and back axles of the garbage truck and knelt beside him to feel through the man's pockets for a wallet or some form of identification. His pockets were empty but for a packet of cigarettes. It wouldn't do any good to take a photo of the guy with his head crushed.

Dev pushed the man's right sleeve up, searching for any kind of identifying marks. Nothing. When he pushed the left sleeve up, he found a Polynesian mask inked in black on the inside of the man's forearm. He quickly snapped a photo of the tattoo with his cell phone.

The truck driver dropped out of the driver's seat. "I couldn't stop," he said, his voice shaking. "Is he…?"

"Dead?" Dev nodded. He didn't have to feel for a pulse. The garbage truck's wheel had rolled over the man's skull, crushing it beneath its massive weight.

"Sweet Jesus," the truck driver muttered, fumbling in his pocket. "We need to call 911."

Another man approached, his cell phone pressed to his ear. "I just placed a call to 911. They're sending someone now."

The truck driver quit digging for his phone and ran his hand through his dark hair. "I've never run over a man before. Did you know him? Was he a friend?"

Dev straightened, shaking his head. "No. I don't know him. And no, he wasn't a friend. He assaulted a woman. Excuse me." He stepped away from the truck, the driver and the good Samaritan reporting the accident.

"Sir, you're not leaving, are you?" the truck driver called out.

"Not yet," Dev responded.

"Good, 'cause you're the main witness." The distraught garbageman stared down at the dead man, frowning worriedly. "The police are going to want to talk to you."

"I need to check on the woman this guy attacked." He hadn't wanted to leave Kiana alone. Now that Tish's attacker was neutralized, he was anxious to get back to the women. This man was dead, but that didn't mean he was the only one who could hurt Kiana and Tish.

After Kiana's phone rang three times, Dev was getting worried.

"Dev," she finally answered. "Where are you? Are you all right? Did you catch him?"

He was so relieved to hear her voice that he had to take a breath before answering, "I'm several blocks away from the apartment building. I'm all right, but Tish's attacker isn't. How's Tish?"

"I'm worried about her. She's nonresponsive. The paramedics are working with her now, loading her into an ambulance. I'm going to ride with her to the hospital. What do you mean the attacker isn't all right?"

"He's dead."

"Holy shit," Kiana murmured. "Did you..."

Dev shook his head, his lips quirking on the corners. "No. I didn't kill him. He ran out into a busy street and was hit by a garbage truck."

"Oh, thank God," Kiana said. "The bastard deserved to die."

"Yeah," he agreed. "Only it's too bad we couldn't question him first."

"Do you know who he is?" she asked. "Was there any form of identification on him?"

"I felt in his pockets," Dev said. "He wasn't carrying an ID."

"Okay, I'm coming." Kiana's voice sounded distant, as if she was talking to someone else away from her phone. Then she came back to him with, "Look, the ambulance is getting ready to leave. I have to go."

Dev's gut knotted. If she left the apartment, she'd be even further away from him than she was at that moment. "Are you going to be all right?" he asked. "I'll have to stay and talk with the police."

"I'll be okay. Police are crawling all over the apartment. I'll be safe in the ambulance. Can you meet me at the Queens Medical Center when you free up?"

"I will. And Kiana, stay with people," Dev said. "We don't know if this man was working for someone else. He attacked Tish. Whoever sent him might come after you next."

"I'll be okay until you get to me," she said. "Just hurry." The call ended.

Dev stared down at the phone, wishing he could go to Kiana immediately.

He had a really bad feeling in his gut about what had just happened.

Through all the years he'd spent on active duty and all the missions he'd been involved with, his gut feelings had never been wrong.

Kiana's Hero (#3)

ABOUT THE AUTHOR

ELLE JAMES also writing as MYLA JACKSON is a *New York Times* and *USA Today* Bestselling author of books including cowboys, intrigues and paranormal adventures that keep her readers on the edges of their seats. When she's not at her computer, she's traveling, snow skiing, boating, or riding her ATV, dreaming up new stories. Learn more about Elle James at www.ellejames.com

Website | Facebook | Twitter | GoodReads | Newsletter | BookBub | Amazon

Or visit her alter ego Myla Jackson at mylajackson.com
Website | Facebook | Twitter | Newsletter

Follow Me!
www.ellejames.com
ellejamesauthor@gmail.com

ALSO BY ELLE JAMES

Gerard (#2)

Lucas (#3)

Beau (#4)

Rafael (#5)

Valentin (#6)

Landry (#7)

Simon (#8)

Maurice (#9)

Jacques (#10)

Brotherhood Protectors Yellowstone

Saving Kyla (#1)

Saving Chelsea (#2)

Saving Amanda (#3)

Saving Liliana (#4)

Saving Breely (#5)

Saving Savvie (#6)

Saving Jenna (#7)

Saving Peyton (#8)

Saving Londyn (#9)

Brotherhood Protectors Colorado

SEAL Salvation (#1)

Rocky Mountain Rescue (#2)

Iron Horse Legacy

Up in Flames (#6)

Total Meltdown (#7)

Take No Prisoners Series

SEAL's Honor (#1)

SEAL'S Desire (#2)

SEAL's Embrace (#3)

SEAL's Obsession (#4)

SEAL's Proposal (#5)

SEAL's Seduction (#6)

SEAL'S Defiance (#7)

SEAL's Deception (#8)

SEAL's Deliverance (#9)

SEAL's Ultimate Challenge (#10)

Texas Billionaire Club

Tarzan & Janine (#1)

Something To Talk About (#2)

Who's Your Daddy (#3)

Love & War (#4)

Billionaire Online Dating Service

The Billionaire Husband Test (#1)

The Billionaire Cinderella Test (#2)

The Billionaire Bride Test (#3)

The Billionaire Daddy Test (#4)

The Billionaire Matchmaker Test (#5)

The Billionaire Glitch Date (#6)

The Billionaire Perfect Date (#7) coming soon

The Billionaire Replacement Date (#8) coming soon

The Billionaire Wedding Date (#9) coming soon

Cajun Magic Mystery Series

Voodoo on the Bayou (#1)

Voodoo for Two (#2)

Deja Voodoo (#3)

Cajun Magic Mysteries Books 1-3

The Outriders

Homicide at Whiskey Gulch (#1)

Hideout at Whiskey Gulch (#2)

Held Hostage at Whiskey Gulch (#3)

Setup at Whiskey Gulch (#4)

Missing Witness at Whiskey Gulch (#5)

Cowboy Justice at Whiskey Gulch (#6)

Boys Behaving Badly Anthologies

Rogues (#1)

Blue Collar (#2)

Pirates (#3)

Stranded (#4)

66059698R00161